The
Wand

THE HAGSTONE CHRONICLES
BOOK THREE

MAVIS GULLIVER

INDEPENDENT INNOVATIVE INTERNATIONAL

Published by Cinnamon Press,
Meirion House,
Tanygrisiau,
Blaenau Ffestiniog,
Gwynedd LL41 3SU
www.cinnamonpress.com

The right of Mavis Gulliver to be identified as author of this work
has been asserted by her in accordance with the Copyright, Designs
and Patent Act, 1988. © 2016 Mavis Gulliver.
ISBN 978-1-910836-22-4
British Library Cataloguing in Publication Data. A CIP record for
this book can be obtained from the British Library.

Designed and typeset in Palatino and Lucida by Cinnamon Press.
Cover design by Adam Craig based on a design by Christopher Hull
for 'Cry at Midnight' from original artwork 'Moonlight Horse' by
Destinyvispro © agency: Dreamstime.com

Cinnamon Press is represented by Inpress and by the Welsh Books
Council in Wales. Printed in Poland

Acknowledgements

Grateful thanks to Jan Fortune and everyone at Cinnamon Press for publishing *The Hagstone Chronicles*. *Cry at Midnight* in 2014, *Clickfinger* in 2015 and *The Snake Wand* in 2016. Thanks to Christopher Hull for the original cover design and Adam Craig for a great cover depicting both McCaig's Tower in Oban and The Snake Wand.

Without my grandchildren I would not have written *The Snake Wand*. So thanks to them for reading *Cry at Midnight* and *Clickfinger* and for saying, with genuine enthusiasm – 'Granny, you can't stop there.' A special thank you to Cerys for suggesting a stone spell, and to Olive for giving me the silver-sequined purse that was exactly what I needed for Sula's Token.

Thanks to Caryl, Mary, Pat and Annette for helpful comments and proof-reading.

There aren't enough words to thank Richard, my husband, for living with my stories and taking me to the locations that inspired them. A sense of place is vitally important to me so I thank Scotland for providing inspiring settings for the action in my books. All the adventures on Earth happen in real places, so you, my readers, can walk where Merryn, Hamish and the other children walked; and even if you never visit the locations, you will gain a picture of what they are truly like. The Land of Benevolent Wizardry came from my imagination. Like me, you can only visit it in your dreams.

Further information including photographs of locations and magical tokens can be found on my website, mavisgulliver.co.uk and on Facebook pages 'The Hagstone Chronicles', 'Cry at Midnight', 'Clickfinger' and 'The Snake Wand'.

For my grandchildren
Olive, Josef and Cerys

The Snake Wand

Chapter 1

The woman peered through half-closed eyes. 'Hamish MacQueen,' she said. 'I know all about you. You—and your pest of a sister.'

Hamish backed away. Instinctively his hand slipped into his pocket to clutch the yellow crystal. Normally it felt warm to his touch. Now it was as cold as ice—a sure sign that this was no ordinary woman. Despite her neat appearance she was definitely a witch.

'Merryn.' His voice rose to a desperate shout. 'Merryn.'

'It's no use shouting for help,' said the witch who had disguised herself as a perfectly ordinary woman. 'There's no one here except you—and me. Your sister cycled to the slipway to meet your parents from the ferry. She won't be back for ages.'

A shiver threaded its way down Hamish's back. The witch must know about Merryn's necklace of sea-beans and hag-stones. She must know that he was only safe if he was close to Merryn's side. But how did she know? She must have been spying on them, listening to them, watching them, biding her time until he was alone. He pushed the door, trying with all his might to shut the witch out, but she stuck out her foot and stopped the door from closing.

'Go away,' he shouted.

The witch peered through the gap and laughed. 'There's no need to be unfriendly,' she said. 'I only want to come inside.'

'Well you can't.' He leaned on the door and stamped on the toe of the witch's shoe. 'Go away. I don't talk to strangers.'

'Nonsense,' said the witch. 'I'm not a stranger. I'm Veronica Smythe. Your parents rent this cottage from me so I have the right to come in.'

Hamish kicked at the leg that poked through the widening gap, but it was no use. Veronica Smythe gave one tremendous push. The door flew open. He was knocked aside and the witch barged in. He started to follow her, but soon changed his mind. She could stay in the house on her own. He must find Merryn so that she could tell The Benevolent Wizards that another witch had arrived on the island. He turned to the door, but it slammed before he reached it. He tried to open it, but it was locked as firmly as if someone had turned a key. He dashed to the back door, but that too was locked. A scornful laugh brought him to a shuddering stop. He was trapped and all he could do was watch as the witch poked her nose into every corner of the room. When she opened the desk and began rifling through papers, Hamish's fear turned to anger.

'How dare you?' he shouted. 'Those belong to my dad.'

'Then tell me where it is,' she said. 'It isn't in Gylen Castle so it must be here.'

'I...I don't know what you're... t...talking about,' he stuttered.

But even as he spoke two things raced into his mind. Firstly, the witch's initials were V S—the same as for Vitriola Sniff. Secondly, she must be searching for The Book of Spells because that was the only thing left behind when Ammonia Clickfinger's magic unravelled. It was the book that lay hidden inside a shoe-box on the top shelf of Merryn's wardrobe.

Veronica Smythe sniffed her way upstairs. 'It's here,' she said. 'I can smell it.'

Hamish followed, but the longer he stayed close to her, the colder his yellow crystal grew. He watched helplessly as she opened the wardrobe, grabbed the box and pulled out The Book of Spells.

'At last,' she cried, 'Clickfinger's spells will increase my power. Now I'll get the better of Mandragora.'

'Never,' called a triumphant voice.

Hamish whipped round and gasped at the sight of a witch who hadn't bothered to disguise herself. It was Mandragora Twitch and she was reaching for The Book of Spells.

Instantly, Veronica Smythe transformed herself into Vitriola Sniff. 'No,' she screeched. 'I found it. It's mine.'

Hamish shrank back as the witches began a battle for possession. There were no wands. There was nothing like Ammonia's terrifying black finger. There was nothing as powerful as The Snake Wand. If it hadn't been so serious Hamish would have laughed because it was a battle of noses. Now he could see why their names were Sniff and Twitch. As they stared at one another their faces grimaced and wrinkled. Vitriola sniffed through her long wart-bedecked nose while the tip of Mandragora's nose twitched up and down like the nose of a particularly ugly rabbit.

Vitriola held on to The Book of Spells. She swung it from side to side as she tried to avoid Mandragora's magic, but an extra strong twitch from Mandragora's nose tossed the book into the air. In their rush to catch it, the two witches collided. Vitriola fell face down and Mandragora collapsed on top of her. The book landed behind them. Hamish dashed forwards and in the split of a second he had it in his hand.

Quickly he threw Merryn's duvet, two pillows and a chair on top of the struggling witches. He leaned against the bed and pushed until they were trapped between the bed and the wall. Then he slammed the door and ran downstairs. He dashed back and forth, tugging at door handles, and desperately trying to open windows, but there was no escape. He slumped in a chair and clutched The Book of Spells to his chest.

Thoughts whirled inside his head. When the witches found their feet they'd come after him. They'd trap him. One of them would take the book. It didn't matter which one. They were both Malevolent Witches and either one of them would use it in the fight against Benevolent Wizardry.

From upstairs came the sound of bangs and scrapes as the bed was pushed aside. Vitriola's high-pitched screams mixed with Mandragora's deeper shouts as the witches hurled insults at one another. Hamish flinched when he heard the thud of feet as the witches jostled their way downstairs. He looked round wildly. There wasn't a moment to lose. The wood-burning stove caught his eye. As the witches burst into the room he opened the door and threw The Book of Spells inside. There was a sudden flare as it burst into flames. The witches stared in horror as dirty grey smoke billowed into the room.

'You stupid boy,' Mandragora yelled.

Vitriola turned on Mandragora. 'It's your fault,' she screeched. 'If you hadn't followed me it would have been mine. Now it's lost forever.'

Sniffs and twitches began all over again and this time Hamish couldn't help laughing. 'You're the stupid ones,' he said. 'You spend your time arguing and keeping secrets. If you worked together...' He slapped his hand over his mouth as the witches stopped and stared at one another.

'The boy is right,' said Mandragora.

'He means two brains are better than one,' said Vitriola.

'Exactly,' said Mandragora. 'Besides, fighting is wearing me out. Let's co-operate. Thanks, Hamish MacQueen. I'll never forgive you for burning The Book of Spells, but if Vitriola and I work together we probably won't need it.'

Vitriola grinned. 'Here's to a partnership and high fives to clinch it.'

The witches hooted with malicious laughter. Their hands met in a resounding slap and they disappeared. Hamish tried to slow his panting breath. The witches had gone, but signs of their presence were everywhere. He flung open both doors, hoping that a draught would blow away the stench that they'd left behind. He rushed round, replacing things that Vitriola had moved. He tidied the desk and ran up to Merryn's room to clear the mess that had been made by the struggle.

He hadn't quite finished when his dad's Land Rover pulled up outside. From the window he watched as Merryn lifted her bike out of the back. He picked up the chair and threw the pillows and duvet back onto the bed, but he didn't have time to close the wardrobe before Merryn ran upstairs.

'Hamish MacQueen, you little sneak,' she cried. 'What are you doing in my room?'

Hamish covered his face with his hands and let out a long slow breath. He listened to Merryn ranting about there being no excuse, about breaking rules, about how she'd never trust him again. He let his hands fall and his voice shook when he finally managed to answer.

'I can explain. Only I don't think you'll believe me.'

Chapter 2

Merryn stood in her bedroom, hands on hips, glaring at Hamish. 'I'm waiting for an explanation,' she said, 'and it had better be a good one.'

Hamish hesitated. He didn't know where to begin. He looked at the floor then he looked up at the wardrobe. Merryn followed his glance and saw that the door was ajar. She ran across the room, pulled the shoebox from the top shelf, opened it and turned angrily.

'Where is it? What have you done with it? We agreed to hide it until we could give it to Tobias.'

Hamish lowered his head and mumbled through his fingers. 'I burnt it.'

Merryn's gasp was followed by a scream. 'You did what?'

'Don't scream at me.' Hamish glared at her. 'I burnt it and you'd have done the same if you'd been here. Only if you had been here none of it would have happened.'

The horror of his recent encounter suddenly overwhelmed him. 'I didn't know what else to do,' he wailed. His face crumpled. He threw himself on the bed and buried his face in the pillow.

Merryn's heart began to thump. She shouldn't have left him on his own. Something awful had happened and she hadn't been there to protect him. She flopped down and put her arm round him. 'You'd better tell me what happened,' she said.

'Vitriola Sniff,' he mumbled. 'She knew about The Book of Spells. She couldn't find it in the castle so she came here. She knows all about you so she waited until you'd gone out.'

He sat up and rubbed his eyes. 'But how did she know where to find me? And how did she know we had anything to do with Clickfinger? I don't understand.'

'Neither do I,' said Merryn. She shuddered at the thought of a witch coming into her bedroom, but she pushed the feeling away. 'I expect she followed her nose. It's certainly long enough.'

Hamish sniffed and gave the faintest of grins. 'You're right. She said she could smell the book. Then Mandragora Twitch came and they fought over it and I threw it in the stove. They called me stupid. I lost my temper and said they were the stupid ones, spending all their time arguing and keeping secrets. I said that if they worked together they'd...'

'You didn't,' Merryn gasped. 'Please tell me you didn't.'

'I did,' said Hamish, 'and they knew what I meant. They did a high five and disappeared together like the best of friends.'

At the sight of his worried face Merryn stopped herself from ranting about his stupidity. 'Well, at least they didn't get the book. It was the only thing that Clickfinger left behind. So it really is the end of her horrible magic.'

'I don't think so,' said Hamish. 'When she was eliminated her clothes didn't disappear.'

'They don't matter,' said Merryn. 'Emily and the other children made them. There was no magic involved. That's why they weren't destroyed.'

'I know that,' said Hamish,' but think about it. Inside McCaig's Tower, the hall with its stage and everything disappeared because it was made by magic. But anything that wasn't made by magic stayed behind.'

Merryn nodded. 'Yes, like The Book of Spells in Gylen Castle.'

'And what about Clickfinger's locket?' Hamish asked. 'I don't think she made that by magic. I bet it's still there.'

Merryn gasped. She knew that Ammonia kept The Great Wizard's hair inside her locket. One hair had been used to materialise The Great Wizard, but what if there'd been more than one? If the witches found the locket with another hair inside they would still have power over The Great Wizard.

'I've got to tell Tobias,' she said.

She grasped her pink crystal and waited anxiously for Tobias to answer her call. Hamish wandered across to the window and looked out. Disgruntled that he wouldn't be able to hear the wizard's words, he drummed impatiently on the windowsill.

Merryn, frustrated by the long wait, thought about Kester. She wished she could speak to him, but until he became a fully-fledged wizard all contact was forbidden. It was a hard rule to obey, but she knew that if the witches intercepted their call, they could both be tracked down. It was a risk she couldn't take. Minutes ticked away. She'd almost given up hope of a reply when a voice cut into her thoughts.

'I apologise for the delay,' said Tobias. 'I was at the Awards Ceremony where Kester received his prize. He is our top student and very soon he will graduate as a Full Wizard.'

'That's brilliant,' she said. 'I can't wait to speak to him, but you must listen. Awful things have happened. Two witches came and…'

'Calm yourself,' said Tobias. 'Tell me all. Start at the beginning.'

So Merryn poured out the tale while Hamish bit his lip and tried not to interrupt. She explained how she'd found The Book of Spells in Gylen Castle, and how, in the excitement of seeing Kester again, she'd forgotten to give it to him. She told him how Vitriola Sniff and Mandragora Twitch had come to the cottage and how Hamish had burned the book.

Tobias listened patiently. 'Do not worry about burning The Book of Spells,' he said. 'It is true that we could have made use of it, but at least it has not fallen into the wrong hands. Tell Hamish that he did well.'

'But that's not all,' said Merryn. 'Twitch and Sniff have made friends and they're going to work together.'

'That is the last thing I expected to hear,' said Tobias, 'but it may be to our advantage. I do not think the partnership will last. Twitch will expect to be in charge and Sniff will be resentful. I predict that they will grow to hate one another even more than before. Then, if fortune is on our side, they will eliminate one another.'

'But there's something else,' said Merryn. 'I think it's the most serious thing of all. Hamish thinks that Ammonia's locket is still in McCaig's Tower.'

A startled cry was followed by silence. Merryn's eyebrows knotted together as she waited anxiously for a reply.

'What's he saying?' Hamish demanded.

Merryn put her finger to her lips and shook her head. 'Nothing at the moment, but he said you did well to burn the book. Now hush. I need to listen.'

But Tobias was not speaking. She sensed that he was thinking deeply about this latest piece of information. In her mind's eye she could see his long fingers stroking his beard as he considered the alternatives.

'If Hamish is right,' Tobias said at last, 'this is grave news indeed. You must search immediately. If other witches have the same thought, they too will be seeking the locket. The Grand High Witch was only concerned with unravelling Clickfinger's spells. The locket was a family heirloom handed to Ammonia by her father. She did not create it so it will not have been destroyed.'

'We know that,' said Merryn with growing impatience. 'The Book of Spells belonged to him too. That's why it was left in Gylen Castle.'

'But perhaps,' Tobias continued, 'you are unaware that the locket is far more than a piece of jewellery. If it contains The Great Wizard's hair it can be used against him. But it also holds the power of The Clickfinger Clan. If another witch finds it and unlocks its secrets she will add The Clickfinger Power to her own. She will be a formidable enemy. Her power may even match that of The Grand High Witch and The Snake Wand.'

Merryn gulped. 'It's worse than I imagined. What are you going to do?'

There was no immediate answer. All she heard was a long drawn out sigh.

'Regretfully, nothing,' said Tobias at last. 'Saving The Great Wizard took the combined strength of all our wizards. We are exhausted and time will pass before we regain our full powers.'

'But it's serious,' Merryn spluttered. 'You said so yourself. You can't just stand back and let the witches find it.'

'In my present state,' said Tobias, 'If I come to McCaig's Tower and meet with Sniff or Twitch I will be vanquished. There is only one way forward. You and Hamish must go. You must find the locket. Take care of Hamish. Tell him to carry the hag-stones and crystals that I left for the other children. They will give additional protection, but he must stay close to you at all times. When you find the locket, you must contact me. Then we will arrange a meeting so that you can give it into my keeping.'

'But...' Merryn opened her mouth to protest. 'We can't. We...' Her words petered out. The crystal had lost its warm glow. Tobias had gone and although she begged him to come back, she didn't hear his voice again.

Chapter 3

Locked, each in their own thoughts, Merryn and Hamish sat in silence. Merryn pondered on their Tiree adventures when they'd sneaked out of Aunt Aggie's house to follow their quest through the hours of darkness. Now Tobias expected them to go to McCaig's tower. But that was in Oban, and Oban was on the mainland.

Hamish began to grumble. 'I don't see why he's leaving it all to us. In any case, we can't do anything tonight. We can't get there and back before the last ferry. We're stumped and it's all your fault for having The Gift.'

'Don't say that,' said Merryn. 'You know I can't help it. I wish I didn't have it, but I'm stuck with it so I have to use it. I've got to help the fight against evil, but you're lucky, you have a choice. You can back out any time.'

'Sorry,' said Hamish. 'I didn't mean it. I want to help, but sometimes the wizards seem to expect too much.'

Merryn nodded in agreement. 'I know what you mean, but we'll find a way. We'll go tomorrow and we'll find the locket – if it's still there.'

'Only if mum and dad let us go,' said Hamish, 'but I bet they won't.'

'Leave it to me,' said Merryn and she ran downstairs to ask.

Hamish went to his room. He tried to read but curiosity got the better of him. He tiptoed downstairs and stood outside the door, straining his ears to catch the conversation. It didn't sound promising, but eventually Merryn came out with a smile on her face. She hustled him into her bedroom and closed the door behind him.

'Mum didn't want us wandering about the town, but dad was great. He phoned the Leisure Centre and booked a day pass. It'll be brilliant. There's a swimming pool with a flume and tennis and…'

'We won't have time for all that,' said Hamish. 'We've got to find the locket. Or have you forgotten?'

Merryn frowned. 'If we go on the first ferry, we can find it and have the rest of the day to enjoy ourselves.'

It was hard to believe that only one day had passed since they'd escaped from Gylen Castle, only one day since The Grand High Witch had used The Snake Wand to eliminate Ammonia Begonia Clickfinger. So much had happened in such a short time, and it wasn't over yet. There were things to do besides searching for Ammonia's locket. There were crystals to give to the three children who'd played such an important part in defeating the witch. There was green for James, blue for Emily and orange for Peter. But the children had vanished and there were few clues as to their whereabouts. Merryn took out her notebook and Hamish peered over her shoulder and read her notes aloud.

'James Henry Watson and Peter - brothers - phone 0163. That's our best clue. I think it might be an Oban number so they may be fairly close. Emily Elizabeth Carmichael - 31.'

'Thirty-one isn't a clue at all,' said Merryn. 'It must be a house number, but it could be anywhere. We'll never find her and it's a shame because I'm sure we could be best friends.'

'And don't forget the others,' said Hamish.

'I'll never forget them,' said Merryn, 'but I don't think we'll find them. Clickfinger could have brought them from the other side of Scotland for all we know.'

She ticked them off on her fingers. 'Emily, James, Peter, Rosie, Ben, Heather, Hazel, Justin, Megan and Lisa, that's it. Ten altogether.'

'But what do we say when we do find them?' Hamish asked. 'Tobias said they won't remember anything. So if we start talking about witches and being turned into spiders and slugs and big fat pigs they'll think we're mad.'

'I know,' said Merryn, 'but they need protecting so we've got to give them the hag-stones. We'll know what to say when the time comes.'

'I hope you're right,' said Hamish, 'but before we do anything else we'd better protect the cottage. If we'd done that as soon as we got home Veronica Smythe wouldn't have got in.'

Merryn raised her eyebrows. 'Who?'

'Veronica Smythe,' he said. 'Didn't I tell you? That beastly Sniff came in disguise. She looked perfectly normal until Twitch showed up. Then she changed into her horrible witchy self.'

Merryn sighed in exasperation. 'No, you didn't tell me. What else have you missed out?'

'Nothing,' said Hamish. 'Come on. Where are the hag-stones? You must have taken them with you when you went to meet the ferry. If you'd left them here those beastly witches wouldn't have got past them and I'd have been safe.'

'I'm sorry,' said Merryn. 'They're in my saddlebag. We'd better get them now.'

From the bike shed she took the bundle that Tobias had given her. She put her hand inside and when she brought it out, she was holding four hag-stones.

'Four for the corners,' said Hamish. 'Let's bury them right away.'

It didn't take long. Hamish dug out plugs of turf. Merryn put the hag-stones in and Hamish covered them. For the second time Merryn slipped her hand inside the bag. This time she was holding three larger hag-stones.

'Two for the doors,' said Hamish, 'but why three?'

'No idea,' said Merryn.

While they were burying the two hag-stones she wondered what to do with the third one. Maybe it was to keep witches out of the garage, or perhaps it was to protect the bike shed.

'Let's put it outside the garden gate,' said Hamish, 'although it won't stop the witches from climbing over the fence. Next time we go to the shore we'd best search for more. Then we can put them all round the garden.'

'Good plan,' said Merryn. 'Now, let's see if we can find James.'

After fifteen minutes of squinting at small print in the Argyll Telephone Directory they began to see that it wasn't going to be easy. Without a complete area code and without parents' initials they would have to phone hundreds of Watsons. So they left it for the time being and packed their bags for the next day's trip to Oban.

When everything was ready, Merryn took out her pink crystal in the hopes of speaking to Tobias. He must have been waiting for her call, because his answer came quickly and his voice was eager.

'You've found it.'

'No, we haven't. We haven't even looked. McCaig's Tower is on the mainland. We're on an island. We can't just walk there. We have to catch a ferry.'

'Whatever the problems, you must overcome them. You must go now,' said Tobias.

Merryn clenched her fists in frustration. 'We can't. Don't you understand? It's too late. It's our bedtime soon and there isn't another ferry tonight.'

The wizard's voice wavered with anxiety. 'This is unfortunate. It is a matter of extreme urgency. If you cannot go now you must go at first light tomorrow.'

'We'll go on the first ferry,' she said, 'but what if we're too late? What if the witches have already found the locket?'

'If that has happened,' said Tobias, 'Benevolent Wizardry is in greater peril than ever. I dare not consider the consequences.'

'And what do I do about Hamish?' she asked. 'I can't keep him close to me all the time. The holidays are nearly over. We'll be at school in different classes. I won't see him for hours on end. Sniff and Twitch know who he is and they said they'd never forgive him for burning The Book of Spells.'

She paused while she sorted out her thoughts. 'It's strange they didn't do anything to him when they had the chance. If they wanted to punish him, why didn't they do it there and then?'

'I am not sure,' said Tobias, 'but they may have plans to capture him so that they can blackmail you.'

Merryn's breath caught in her throat. 'But…'

'Calm yourself. I am not saying that will happen. I am simply warning you. I will find a way of protecting your brother, but it may take time. In the meantime, you must not let him out of your sight.'

Tobias didn't speak again. Merryn dropped the crystal on the bed and put her head in her hands.

Hamish shook her by the shoulder. 'What did he say?'

'He said to remind you that my necklace is your only real protection. As long as you're inside the bubble with me you'll be OK. He said that Sniff and Twitch will be watching you and they'll stop at nothing to get hold of the locket.'

Chapter 4

Merryn and Hamish headed through the streets of Oban towards the steps that led to McCaig's Tower.

'A hundred and forty-four,' Hamish called as he reached the top. 'Come on, slow coach, we haven't got all day.'

From the end of the path Merryn looked up at the arched entrance with its castellated top.

'I don't like it,' she said. 'I suppose it's all right in daylight, but I can't help thinking about the Festival of Malevolent Witchery. All those witches inside and every one of them pointing their wands at The Great Wizard.'

'Not just wands,' said Hamish, 'noses and fingers and whatever else they use to make their beastly magic. And worst of all, The Snake Wand with its frightful flickering tongue. That's the one that really freaks me out. I hope I never have to look at it again.'

'Well it isn't here now,' said Merryn, 'so come on, let's find the locket then we can go swimming.'

Hamish reached the arch first but he quickly turned back. He gave an enormous shudder and pushed his hand into his pocket.

'My crystal feels cool,' he said, 'and I think I saw Veronica Smythe—Vitriola Sniff in disguise.'

'And my necklace is starting to throb.' said Merryn. 'Bother! That means she got here before us.'

Hamish peered cautiously round the stonework and dipped back again. 'There's another woman with her. It must be Mandragora Twitch. They're poking about under the bushes. What are we going to do?'

Merryn shrugged. 'There's only one thing we can do. We've got to find the locket before they do.'

'But…'

'But nothing.' Merryn grasped him firmly by the hand. 'We have no choice.'

Hamish tried to pull away. 'Stop struggling,' she said, 'as long as there are witches about I'm holding on to you. You have to stay inside the bubble,'

Hamish scowled, but he allowed Merryn to lead him into the Tower. They knew at once that finding the locket in such a large space would be difficult. Besides, the two witches were already searching. They were on their hands and knees in the middle of the Tower, their long noses sniffing and twitching as they tried to discover the locket's hiding place.

Merryn pulled Hamish behind a bush and spoke in a whisper. 'They're searching in the wrong place. Think about it. Clickfinger was on the stage when she was eliminated, but the stage wouldn't have been in the middle of the building. It would have been at one end, like in a theatre. If the locket's still here it's somewhere round the edge.'

Still holding onto Hamish she set off along the path that followed the curve of the tower walls. She watched as a dog ran towards the witches with a low growl rumbling in its throat. A second later, it yelped and ran back to its owner with its tail between its legs.

'See,' she said as she tightened her grip on Hamish's hand. 'That's why you have to stay with me.'

Suddenly, the quiet space was filled with chattering as a coach load of tourists came through the archway. Shortly afterwards they were followed by a woman with three children, then by an elderly gentleman and lastly by half a dozen boys with a football.

'Great,' she said. 'With so many people about, there's less chance of the witches noticing us.'

They walked slowly round the tower, and as they reached the far side the necklace of sea-beans and hagstones began to throb. A few steps farther on it gave an enormous jolt.

'This is it,' she said. 'My necklace knows it's here.'

Her eye caught a length of chain poking out from the grass at the edge of the path. Before she could reach it, Hamish pulled his hand out of hers and picked it up.

'Yes,' he cried as he swung the locket on its chain.

Instantly she clapped her hand over his mouth, but the witches had heard his cry. They looked up, recognised him and scrambled to their feet. Merryn snatched the locket, pushed it in her pocket, grabbed his hand again and ran. She didn't stop to see what the witches were doing, but she heard a voice ringing out across the tower.

'Hamish McQueen, come back at once. If you don't, you'll be sorry.'

Down the steps and through the town they raced, weaving in and out of the crowds. They dodged between people who were taking photographs and people who were wandering along as if they had all the time in the world. On they ran until they were safely inside the Leisure Centre. Out of breath, but relieved to have given the witches the slip, Merryn gave her name and explained about the day pass.

'I've got to speak to Tobias,' she said as they paused by the men's changing room door. 'Whatever you do, don't come out until I knock like this.' She tapped, rat tat rat-a-tat tat. Lowering her voice to a whisper she added, 'I don't think they followed us, but we can't be too careful.'

Leaving Hamish, she went into the women's changing room. In the moment between snatching the locket and pushing it into her pocket she hadn't looked at it. Now, as she placed it in her palm it began to vibrate. At the same time, the necklace of sea-beans and hag-stones increased its throbbing. She tried to look away from the locket, but eyes of blue crystal drew her back. They stared at her from the face of a long-eared owl, a face engraved on a bronze circle. With a shudder, she closed her eyes so that those of the owl could no longer burn into hers. But there was no getting away from the sinister vibrations. Until she could give it to Tobias, she was stuck with it. It was her responsibility to keep it safe from the witches—and there was no one to help her.

She pushed it back into her pocket, took out the pink crystal and sent a desperate message to Tobias. To her relief, the wizard replied immediately.

'Merryn, do you have the locket?'

'Yes, but it's scaring me.' Fear and panic made her rush through the words. 'It's got eyes. It's trying to cast a spell on me. Sniff and Twitch know we've got it. We gave them the slip, but I'm sure they're still looking for us.'

'Do not attempt to open it,' said Tobias. 'Neither you nor Hamish must look at it again. Put it round your neck next to the hag-stone and sea-bean necklace. Then keep it hidden inside your clothes.'

Merryn closed her eyes. She fumbled in her pocket, felt for the chain and slipped it over her head. 'All right,' she said. 'I'm wearing it, but the sea-beans and hag-stones don't like it. The locket's vibrating and the necklace is shaking like anything. It's unbearable, it's terrifying, it's...'

'It is necessary,' said Tobias. 'Your necklace is counteracting the evil forces. I am sorry that it is painful for you, but you must bear it for all our sakes. Now tell me where you are.'

'I'm in the women's changing room at the Leisure Centre in Oban.'

'And Hamish?' The wizard's voice was sharp with anxiety. 'Where is Hamish?'

'In the men's changing room.'

'Then find him immediately. I told you not to let him out of your sight. He must stay inside the bubble.'

Merryn gasped. She picked up her bag, ran to the men's changing room and tapped on the door. Rat tat rat-a-tat tat. Hamish didn't come out. She tried again, much louder. Rat Tat Rat-a-Tat Tat.

A young man came out. 'What do you want?' he asked.

'My brother,' said Merryn. 'Hamish McQueen, he went in to get changed and he hasn't come out. Please, can you find him?'

'OK,' said the young man and he went back inside.

Merryn could scarcely breathe. Her heart skipped half a dozen beats. As she waited, the locket sent out more evil vibrations, and the necklace of sea-beans and hag-stones went on thudding against her collarbone.

Chapter 5

'I'm sorry,' said the young man as he came out of the changing room, 'but I can't find anyone called Hamish.'

'But he must be there. He's got to be there. Please look again.'

'There's no point,' said the young man. 'I looked everywhere and there's no sign of him. He must be in the pool already.'

The door closed, but Merryn was too distraught to take no for an answer. She hammered on the door and shouted. 'Hamish, come out at once.'

The girl from the reception desk came over and tapped Merryn on the shoulder. 'You can't carry on like that,' she said. 'What's all the fuss about?'

'My brother,' Merryn gasped. 'He went to get changed but he's disappeared.'

'You must be Merryn MacQueen,' said the girl. 'I've been expecting you.'

Merryn gulped. Sudden fear overwhelmed her. She tried to speak but the words stuck in her throat.

'There's nothing to worry about. Your two aunts came for him. They left a message for you.'

She led Merryn to the desk and handed her a piece of paper. 'Here you are.'

Merryn slumped on a chair and unfolded the paper with trembling fingers.

If you want to see your precious brother again you must bring the locket to McCaig's Tower. Come immediately or you will be too late.

Merryn almost flew out of the door. But which way should she go? Apart from shopping with her mother she'd never had to find her way round the town. Instinct told her that there must be a short cut, but she couldn't be certain. So, for fear of getting lost, she ran back the way she'd come. Back through the crowded streets until, almost blinded by tears of frustration, she reached the foot of the steps.

After a brief pause to catch her breath she began the upward climb. Numbers pounded through her head as she counted in tens. At sixty she doubled over, gasping, but she forced herself to go on. Seventy, eighty, ninety—at a hundred the ache in the back of her knees was almost unbearable. Still she climbed. At a hundred and twenty she had to stop while a group of elderly ladies made their way down to the town. The brief rest made the next few steps a little easier—a hundred and thirty, a hundred and forty, a hundred and forty-four. The steps were behind her, but there was still a way to go.

Jogging now, too breathless to sprint, she finally reached the arch that led into the tower. There, in front of a clump of bushes was Hamish. The two witches, holding him captive by some powerful spell, stood, a small distance away on either side.

Before they found the locket she'd caught a glimpse of them across the tower. That had been scary enough. Coming face to face with them both made her knees wobble, but she stood her ground and glared. Vitriola

Sniff, small and skinny with frizzy grey hair poking from under her steeple hat glared back. Mandragora Twitch, head and shoulders taller than Vitriola threw back her head and gave a malicious laugh. Merryn fixed her eyes on Hamish. She forced herself to walk across the grass and she stopped about ten metres away from him.

'Come closer and give the locket to me,' Mandragora demanded.

'No,' Vitriola shrieked. 'Give it to me. I found it first.'

So an argument began, but however much they yelled at each other, their spell still held Hamish. They argued over his head, each determined to take possession of the locket. It was as Tobias had predicted. If they carried on like this, one of them would overpower the other. As far as Merryn was concerned, the sooner that happened the better it would be. The locket was vibrating ever more strongly. It was as if it was trying to join the argument, as if it was getting angry at the sound of the raised voices.

Merryn tried to concentrate on what she already knew. Clickfinger had hated Sniff and Twitch. In fact all three witches had hated one another with a vengeance. They'd been rivals for the thirteenth chair on The Council of Malevolent Witchery and they were all jealous of each other. Could that old rivalry still be alive inside the locket? If it wasn't, why was the locket starting to buzz like an angry bee? Why was her necklace bouncing about as if the sea-beans had turned into jumping beans? Suddenly she had an idea. With a bit of luck it would save Hamish and stop the witches from winning The Clickfinger Locket.

'Hamish, close your eyes,' she shouted, 'and don't open them until I say it's safe.'

He nodded his head and closed his eyes tightly. Now she was ready to outwit the witches.

'Be quiet,' she ordered at the top of her voice, 'both of you.'

Sniff and Twitch, surprised and shocked by her outburst, stopped and stared.

'Right,' she said. 'What's this about a locket? And what makes you think that I have it?'

Vitriola's mouth fell open as if she couldn't think of an answer.

'Don't think you can fool me,' Mandragora snarled. 'You knew about the locket and you came here to search for it. You found it, you must have. You...' She faltered as if she was no longer sure of the facts.

Merryn spoke calmly.' I don't know what you're talking about. If there is a locket, why do you want it? What's so special about it? Who did it belong to anyway?'

'Clickfinger,' said Vitriola.

The locket jolted.

Mandragora began to laugh.' Ammonia Clickfinger,' she said. 'Remember what happened to her at The Festival. It was hilarious.'

The locket jolted even more fiercely.

Vitriola began to giggle. 'When the Grand High Witch called out Ammonia Begonia Clickfinger, it was the funniest thing I'd ever heard.'

At the mention of Ammonia's full name the locket began to shake with such violence that Merryn almost fainted.

'Don't open your eyes, Hamish,' she gasped.

Her fingers found the embossing on the locket and she turned the owl's face towards the witches. Immediately, two beams of blue light shot from the crystal eyes. They flew over Vitriola's head and sent Mandragora stumbling into the bushes. Vitriola gave a squeal of joy. She ran to snatch the locket, but her hand met the barrier of the bubble and her mouth opened in shocked surprise.

Merryn pushed the locket against the witch's outstretched hand. It didn't seem to matter that the skin of the bubble lay between them. A voice rang out, loud and triumphant. It was the voice of Ammonia Begonia Clickfinger and it came from the locket and called the witch's name.

'Vitriola Pustula Sniff.'

There was barely time for Vitriola to scream. She knew, as all witches know, that a spell combined with a full name is a fatal one. Blue light rippled from the top of her steeple hat to the toe-tips of her black boots. The hat fell from her head, her grey hair turned to white and she faded away to nothing. The spell that held Hamish broke and he ran to stand behind Merryn, his teeth chattering from the cold that had come from his yellow crystal.

Holding the locket in front of her, Merryn turned the face of the owl towards Mandragora. The witch struggled to untangle herself from the bushes. She got to her knees and put up her hands to shield her eyes.

'Here you are,' said Merryn as she walked towards the witch. 'Take the locket. Take the power of The Clickfinger Clan. Make it your own and you'll be almost as powerful as The Grand High Witch.'

Mandragora lifted her cloak to shield herself from the blue flashing eyes.

'Come on,' Merryn coaxed. 'You wanted the locket. Now's your chance to take it.'

But Mandragora had changed her mind. Just before Merryn reached her, she gave a howl of disappointment and disappeared.

'Bother,' said Merryn. 'A few more steps and she'd have gone the same way as Vitriola.'

She pushed the locket back inside her fleece and then, overwhelmed with relief at saving Hamish, she grabbed him and hugged him tight.

'Get off,' he said as he wriggled out of her arms. 'Thanks, but there's no need to go all soppy.'

He shuddered. 'That was scary. I heard your special knock so I left my rucksack to see what you wanted. I opened the door and then it was too late. The rotten witches tried to grab me. They couldn't touch me, so I thought my hag-stone and my crystal were keeping me safe. They weren't though. Two witches together were just too powerful. I'm not sure how they did it, but I seemed to be flying up a long hill.' He turned round and pointed. 'We came in the entrance over there. It was a lot quicker than going through the town.'

He shuddered again. 'The crystal got so cold I was starting to freeze, and that beastly Twitch won't give up. I've got to get my rucksack before she comes back. Come on, let's hurry. We really need those hag-stones.'

Chapter 6

'We can't go back for your rucksack now,' said Merryn. 'I've got to speak to Tobias. I won't feel safe until he's taken The Clickfinger Locket away.'

Now that the worst of their ordeal was over, her fear was fading, but it was replaced by a slow burning anger. Anger at the huge responsibility that Tobias had placed on her, anger at the risks she'd had to take, anger at the locket that buzzed and vibrated around her neck. Most of all, anger at what had happened to Hamish.

She sat down on the grass and took out her pink crystal.

Tobias answered immediately. 'Merryn. I was worried about you. Tell me that all is well.'

'It is now,' she said, 'but it's no thanks to you. I can't do this any more. It's too dangerous. The witches kidnapped Hamish. It was awful. I thought I'd never see him again. I managed to save him but...'

'Tell me you did not give them the locket.' Tobias interrupted.

'Is that all you care about?' she snapped. 'But, no, of course I didn't. I'm not that stupid. I held it out so that the owl's blue eyes were facing them and I tricked them into saying Ammonia's full name. There was a flash of blue light. A voice shouted Vitriola Pustula Sniff and she faded away. Does that mean she's gone for good? Is she dead?'

'She is indeed,' said Tobias, 'and that is excellent news. Now there is one less ambitious witch to worry about, but what of Mandragora Twitch?'

'I tried to persuade her to take the locket. I thought if she touched it, that it would eliminate her too. She must have thought the same because she made a terrible howling noise and then she disappeared.'

'You took a great risk,' said Tobias, 'but you were right to do so. Mandragora Twitch now knows of your power and your bravery. She will be afraid to confront you again.'

'No, she won't,' said Merryn. 'She's not afraid of me. It's The Clickfinger Locket that terrifies her. Once I get rid of it, I bet she'll come back. I'm scared of the locket, but I'm just as scared of her.'

At the mention of Clickfinger, the locket's menacing sound increased. Immediately, the necklace of sea-beans and hag-stones responded.

Merryn groaned. 'I can't stand it,' she wailed. 'The locket is buzzing away and the necklace is jiggling about. It's unbearable. You've got to come and take it away.' She cried out in desperation. 'Now. This minute. In fact, if you don't, I'm... I'm... I'm going to throw it into the sea.'

'No. Do not do that,' Tobias shouted. He lowered his voice and continued. 'I'm sorry, I should not have shouted, but you must not throw it into the sea. That would be foolish in the extreme. There is no knowing who would find it and to what evil purpose it would be turned. You must keep it until I can take it from you. If Sniff is eliminated and Twitch has disappeared it will be safe for me to come. I am on my way.'

Merryn, still holding her pink crystal, closed her eyes and lay on the grass. Tobias was coming. He would take the ghastly locket away. One more witch had been defeated. Hamish was safe. Now she had time to think. She thought about everything that had happened since the night on Tiree when the horse had cried at midnight and disturbed her sleep. The more she thought, the more she knew that some things had to change.

The Gift was hers for all time and it meant that she had to play her part in the fight against evil. She had to wear the necklace of sea-beans and hag-stones because it protected her from witches and it warned her of danger. Fortunately, it was invisible to ordinary mortals so she could wear it all the time without anyone noticing. She'd got so used to it, that it didn't normally bother her. It was at times like this, when malevolent magic was in the air, that it took on a life of its own and reminded her of its purpose.

She sighed, and for the hundredth time, she wished she'd never heard of The Gift or the necklace of sea-beans and hag-stones. It was a pointless wish because she knew that these things could never change. Other things could change though, the pink crystal, for instance. It allowed her to contact Tobias, and that was reassuring, but it was an awkward thing. She had to have it with her all the time, and sometimes she didn't have a pocket to keep it in. Where was she supposed to put it when she went swimming? The same was true for Hamish. He had to carry his yellow crystal because it turned cold to warn him when witches were near. But that was dangerous too. If she hadn't rescued him from Sniff and Twitch he could have frozen to death. Besides, soon they'd be starting school, going across to Oban every day, changing for games. Sometimes they would have to leave the crystals behind—and if a witch came—what then?

Hamish nudged her with his elbow. 'Merryn, look. Here comes Tobias and he isn't on his own.'

Merryn sat up. A tremor ran round the necklace of sea-beans and hag-stones as a group of men came across the grass towards them. To Merryn, they were not in ordinary clothes, for she could see them as they truly were—wizards with serious expressions on their bearded faces, dressed in tunics, close-fitting trousers and leather shoes with upturned toes. Like Tobias, each one wore a sporran. A sporran engraved with the pattern that never ends, the pattern that means that their fight against evil will go on for ever and ever.

'Meet my colleagues,' said Tobias as he grasped Merryn by the hand, 'you too, Hamish. We are mightily relieved to find you unharmed by your encounter with the witches. In view of what you told me,' he continued, 'we believe the locket is more powerful than we previously thought. The only way forward is to destroy it, but I cannot do that on my own.'

'Is that because you haven't got your full power back?' Hamish asked. 'I know you lost some when you saved The Great Wizard. You all did, didn't you? Is that why you've brought your friends?'

'Exactly,' said Tobias. 'Even though our individual power is much reduced, we are hopeful that our combined powers will be sufficient to put an end to The Clickfinger Locket.'

'You shouldn't have said its name,' Merryn gasped as the locket responded. 'You've made it angry and it's taking it out on me. I've got to get rid of it. Now, this very minute.'

'I am sorry,' said Tobias. 'We will act at once. Close your eyes, both of you. Good. Now place the locket face down on the grass.'

As Merryn's hand closed around the locket, the vibrations increased. Although she tried to place it carefully, it leapt from her fingers.

'Leave it,' Tobias commanded. 'Step away and go quickly. Stay outside the tower and I will call you when we have destroyed it.'

Hamish, anxious to collect his rucksack, wanted to go to the Leisure Centre at once, but Merryn stopped him. She was more concerned with what was happening inside the tower. She leant against a tree and waited impatiently. Within a few minutes she knew that the wizards were engaged in a tremendous struggle. Flashes of blue light shot into the sky. They burst through the archways and bounced back from the high walls. There were raised voices too, and although she couldn't make out the words, she could hear tones of anger, surprise and pain. Above them all, the buzz of the locket grew ever louder. The noise increased in pitch until it was a high strident whine that threatened to split her head in two. On and on went the flashes, the shouts, the cries of pain and the endless, endless whine. She covered her ears to block it out, but it was impossible. It was trapped inside her head and she couldn't escape it.

Then there was silence.

Chapter 7

The silence overwhelmed Merryn. It was more terrifying than the noise that had preceded it. She pressed her hand to her chest in an effort to still the pounding of her heart. Where was Tobias? Why didn't he come? She grabbed Hamish by the hand and pulled him towards the arched entrance.

'Let go,' he said. 'We can't go in until Tobias calls.'

Merryn rubbed her hand over her eyes. 'I can't wait any longer. It's been ages. It's all gone wrong. Just listen.'

Hamish cocked his head to one side. 'I can't hear a thing,' he said.

'Exactly,' she said. 'After all the shouting and…' She stopped and sighed. 'I'm sorry. I keep forgetting you can't hear everything that I hear. There's been a battle with shouts and yells and flashes. The locket filled my head with the most awful whining sound. It went on for ages, but all of a sudden it stopped and I don't know why.'

'There's one way to find out,' said Hamish. 'Let's go and see.'

'But,' said Merryn, 'what if the locket won? What if it's still there?' Her voice shook as she tried to put her greatest fear into words. 'What if Tobias is dead? What if they're all dead?'

Hamish shrugged. 'Well, we won't know until we look.'

Cautiously they edged their way through the arch and onto the grass. The tower, wrapped in a blanket of silence, was deserted. It was as if the battle between good and evil had driven ordinary mortals away. Hamish grasped Merryn's arm as they returned to the place where they'd last seen the wizards. They were still there, lying on the grass in a rough circle. To Merryn they were wizards with wands clutched in their hands, their clothes dishevelled, their faces pale. She knelt beside Tobias and shook him gently by the shoulder. There was no response. She grasped his wrist and felt his pulse. It was faint, but steady.

She let out a long sigh of relief. 'He's alive,' she whispered, 'but he's under a spell and I don't know how to break it.'

'With the crystals,' Hamish said, 'and your necklace, but that might not be enough. I'd better go and get my rucksack.'

He turned to leave but she pulled him back. 'No, we must stay together. Let's try these first. They've worked before. Let's hope they work again.'

She slipped off the necklace and placed it over the wizard's head. She put her pink crystal on his chest. Hamish added his yellow one, but Tobias didn't move.

'Look,' said Hamish, 'there's something in his hand.' He reached down and tried to prize the wizard's fingers apart, but they were clenched in a vice-like grip.

'Don't,' Merryn yelled. 'It's the locket. I can see a bit of the chain.' She looked at Hamish with frightened eyes. 'I'm terrified of it and I'm scared of doing the wrong thing. What if I make it worse?'

'You won't,' said Hamish. 'It can't be worse than it is already.'

'It can,' said Merryn. 'I haven't a clue what to do. Besides, look at the wizards, supposing someone sees them?'

'They'll just see what I see, ordinary guys having a snooze,' he said.

He looked up at the sky where dark clouds were swirling. 'I don't think anyone will come. With clouds like those they'll all think it's raining up here.'

Merryn stood up and walked round the circle of wizards. Their power had obviously deserted them and she had no idea how to bring it back. It was too great a challenge, too huge a responsibility. She dropped down on the grass and hid her face in her hands. Inside her chest, something fluttered like a frightened bird and she couldn't stop it. Finding a way of rescuing the wizards was an enormous challenge, and getting rid of the locket was impossible. If nine wizards with nine wands had failed, what hope had she?

She looked at Tobias and knew she had to do something. She couldn't give in. She wouldn't give in. But what had she got to help her? Two crystals and the necklace had failed to wake Tobias, and they were all she had. But maybe there was another way of using them. The necklace was a barrier to witches. It might also be a barrier to the magic of The Clickfinger Locket. After all, she'd been unharmed when the owl's blue eyes had flashed at her.

'Hamish,' she called. 'I've got an idea, but Tobias said you mustn't look at the locket. So hide in the bushes and keep your eyes closed.'

He immediately began to argue. 'But that's not fair, I'm supposed to stay next to you. What if Clickfinger comes back?'

'Then just turn your back,' she snapped, 'and be ready to run back to me if she comes.'

Muttering to himself, Hamish turned and moved a few paces away. Merryn placed the necklace over Tobias's clenched hand. Slowly, the wizard's fingers uncurled to reveal the locket. It lay, still and silent, face down on his palm. With shaking fingers, Merryn moved it away from the wizard. At the same time, her other hand moved the necklace so that the locket continued to lie within the circle of sea-beans and hag-stones.

Tobias stirred. He opened his eyes, stretched and looked around. The other wizards began to move too.

'The locket,' said Tobias. 'Where is the locket?'

'It's here,' said Merryn. 'I've trapped it, but I don't know what to do next.'

The other wizards came close, linked arms and formed a tight circle around the necklace and the locket. Their left hands covered the pendants that hung from chains around their necks. Their right hands held wands that pointed at the bronze disc.

Tobias spoke briefly. 'By the power of all that is good and true, rid the universe of The Clickfinger Locket for ever and ever.'

'For ever and ever,' the wizards called in unison.

From each wand came a continuous stream of clear purple flame. The locket leapt and turned itself over. The blue eyes flashed as it tried to dodge the magic spells, but it couldn't escape from the circle of sea-beans and hag-stones. The wizards held tight to their wands, but the locket fought back. It shone a brilliant blue that grew stronger and stronger until it pushed back the purple rays of the wizards' spells. Exhausted by the effort, Tobias called a halt.

'We are powerless to destroy it,' he said. 'We must make another plan. We need the bag of hag-stones.'

'It's at the Leisure Centre,' said Merryn. 'Hamish left it behind. That's why Click and Twitch were able to put a spell on him.'

'Go together and get it,' said Tobias. 'We will stay to guard the locket.'

'Come on,' said Hamish. 'We don't have to go through the town. We can go the way the witches brought me.'

They ran to the Leisure Centre and when Hamish reached the desk he spoke to the woman behind it. 'I left my bag behind when the w... when the two women came for me. Can I see if it's in the changing room?' he asked.

'Not until I see your pass,' she said.

Merryn swallowed hard in an effort to stop herself from panicking. 'It was a day pass,' she said. 'My dad booked two places by phone. We'd only just arrived when there was an emergency and we had to leave.'

Hamish looked round desperately. 'We're in a hurry,' he said. 'Please let me look.'

Just then, the girl who'd been on duty earlier in the day appeared. 'It's alright,' she said. 'I remember her.' She pointed at Merryn. 'It'd be hard to forget the fuss she made when she couldn't find her brother. Go on, you can go in.'

Hamish dashed into the changing room. He was gone for all of two minutes. It seemed an age to

Merryn. She couldn't keep still. Her hand went up to clutch the necklace of sea-beans and hag-stones, but it wasn't there. It was in McCaig's Tower with Tobias, the other wizards and The Clickfinger Locket.

She could no longer fight the panic that rose in her throat. It threatened to choke her. If a witch came now, she'd be helpless, powerless to keep herself and Hamish safe. It was not until Hamish appeared with the rucksack that she realised she'd been holding her breath.

'What took you so long?' she gasped. 'I thought someone had taken it.'

'No. I just forgot where I'd put it,' he said, 'but I've got it now, so stop fussing. Let's get back to Tobias.'

Chapter 8

The hag-stones inside Hamish's rucksack jolted and rattled as the young MacQueens ran back to McCaig's Tower. The sun beat down, a blackbird sang, and a few herring gulls made lazy circles in the cloudless sky. It felt like a normal summer's day, but once they passed into the tower everything changed.

Clouds hung above the arched windows. No rays of sun penetrated the gloom. No birds sang. The paths were deserted. The only living things were nine wizards sitting in a silent circle around The Clickfinger Locket and the necklace of sea-beans and hag-stones.

As soon as Hamish opened his rucksack, Tobias grasped the bag. He tipped out the bag of crystals that were meant for Emily, James and Peter. He gathered up the hag-stones and placed them in the space between the locket and Merryn's necklace.

He turned to Merryn and Hamish. 'Close your eyes and do not stand too close. Now we will try again.'

The wizards repeated the same procedure, but they could not master The Clickfinger Locket. They shook their heads in despair when Tobias called a halt for the second time.

Over their heads, above the walls of McCaig's Tower, the clouds grew darker. On the grass, within the circle of Merryn's necklace and the loose hag-stones, The Clickfinger Locket lay still. It had turned its face to the ground, almost as if it was exhausted. Or maybe it was resting in order to regain the strength it had lost in the last battle

'Merryn, Hamish,' said Tobias, 'we have failed again. Open your eyes but be ready to close them if the locket turns over.'

Deep in thought, he stroked his beard as he wondered how to proceed. 'I must call for reinforcements,' he said after a long pause. 'That is our only option.'

He closed his eyes as he summoned more wizards, and after an uneasy silence, he spoke again.

'They are on their way, but the locket has a quality that I had not anticipated. If our power had not been impaired we should have won the day. As we are, even in greater numbers, I fear that it will still resist our efforts.'

'Well,' said Hamish, 'I hope you're not keeping it trapped inside Merryn's necklace. She needs it. We both do. We're not safe without it. So if you can't destroy the locket, you'll have to find another way of trapping it.'

Tobias nodded his head and a slow smile spread across his face.

'Hamish, my boy, you are right. Your comment shows a great deal of common sense and more than a small amount of wisdom. It would sap our strength to make a third attempt, but you have suggested another way. When the other wizards arrive, we will follow your advice.'

'Yes!' Hamish punched the air with his fist. He grinned at Merryn. 'See, I do have good ideas, sometimes.'

'Sometimes,' Merryn agreed. 'I'm glad you had that one. I couldn't bear to leave here without my necklace.'

She watched as huge numbers of wizards passed through the arches of the tower. Like a silent army they came to stand in front of Tobias.

'They're waiting for something,' Hamish whispered.

'Not something,' Merryn whispered back, 'someone. I bet it's The Great Wizard.'

As she spoke, an imposing figure strode across the grass. He was a head taller than the other wizards and his silver grey hair exactly matched the hair that Clickfinger had used in her spell against him. His clothes—trousers and tunic were of the richest purple and all along the edge of his matching cloak was the golden pattern that has no end. At his belt was a sporran and round his neck hung a huge crystal pendulum that glittered and sparkled and shone like the brightest star.

Without a word, he joined the nine wizards, and once again there was a linking of arms and a pointing of wands. Merryn and Hamish backed away as the remaining wizards formed another circle around the first, and another and another until every wizard stood poised and ready.

The voice that called out was stronger and deeper than the voice of Tobias. It was the voice of The Great Wizard, but the words that rang out were similar to the words they'd heard before.

'By the power of all that is good and true, imprison The Clickfinger Locket until we can destroy it for ever.'

A muffled curse came from the locket. A flash of blue light shot high into the sky, but before the locket could send out its destructive spell, it was trapped inside a clear, transparent cube.

'It is done,' said The Great Wizard to the surrounding crowd. 'Fall back and return home without delay.'

At his words the wizards drifted silently away. Only The Great Wizard and Tobias stood alongside Merryn and Hamish.

'Come,' said Tobias. 'The Clickfinger Locket cannot harm us now.' He bent down, picked up the cube and held it out for Merryn and Hamish to see.

Hamish shuddered. 'I still don't like it,' he said. 'I like owls, but that one has an evil face. Its eyes scare me.' He looked up at Tobias and asked, 'What are you going to do with it?'

'When our power is fully restored we will find a means of destroying it,' said Tobias as he slipped it into his sporran. 'Until then I will guard it with my life. It must not fall into the hands of the witches. Now, let me introduce you to The Great Wizard.'

'Do you mean Kester's father?' Hamish asked.

'That too,' said The Great Wizard. 'I am honoured to meet you both. Kester has told me a great deal about you.'

He picked up the necklace of sea-beans and hag-stones and placed it around Merryn's neck. 'Do not take it off again, it is yours and we are grateful for the loan of it. Without it our mission would have failed.'

Tobias opened his sporran and handed an amethyst pendulum to Merryn and a smaller amethyst pendant to Hamish.

'These are to replace the crystals that Kester gave you. We have adjusted the magic and increased their power. They will warn you of the presence of evil, not by turning cold, but by gently vibrating. The silver chain means that you can wear them at all times. Your pendulum, Merryn, has other powers too. When the time comes you will know how to use it.'

He turned to Hamish. 'Yours will allow you to see all the magical things that Merryn sees. Once you wear it, you must never take it off. Besides protecting you, it will allow you to contact me directly.'

'Wow! So Merryn won't have to do it for me.'

'She will not,' said Tobias, 'but use it wisely and only in cases of great need.'

'Like when I find another witch,' said Hamish. A frown crossed his face as he dangled the crystal on its chain. 'I can't wear it. Boys don't wear sparkly jewellery.'

'I can't wear it either,' said Merryn, 'at least not in school. Jewellery isn't allowed.'

'That is not a problem,' said The Great Wizard. 'Take one last look. Now put them over your heads and they, and their chains, will become invisible. You will know that they are there, but few people will be able to see them.'

'Not witches?' asked Hamish.

'Especially not witches,' said The Great Wizard. 'Only those you can trust will be able to see them.'

'Like wizards and Fairy Folk and Selkies,' said Merryn.

'And others who are on the side of all that is good and true.' said Tobias.

He bent down and gathered up the loose hag-stones. 'You must give these to the other children and I trust that you have now protected your cottage.'

'Yes,' said Merryn, 'but seven hag-stones came out of the bag. What should we do with the spare one.'

'It is not spare. It is for Gylen Castle,' said Tobias. 'It will prevent another witch from residing there.'

He opened the bag that held the three crystals, but when he emptied them into Merryn's hand, they too had changed to amethyst pendants.

'You must persuade Emily, James and Peter to wear them,' he said. 'They have exactly the same qualities as the one I gave to Hamish.'

'But we don't know where they live,' said Merryn. 'We might never find them.'

'Keep looking,' said Tobias, 'and you will.'

The Great Wizard suspended his crystal pendulum from his finger. There was a flash of rainbow light and both he and Tobias vanished. The clouds lifted. The sun shone from a clear blue sky. A crowd of chattering children came into the tower and from the tallest tree a thrush began to sing.

'I guess that's the end of that,' said Hamish as he shoved the bag of hag-stones and crystals into his rucksack. 'I don't want to hear another word about witches. We've got one week of the holiday left and I'm going to enjoy it.'

'Me too,' said Merryn. 'As soon as we've buried the hag-stone at the entrance to Gylen Castle I won't give magic another thought.'

Chapter 9

'Merryn is new to the school,' said Mrs Jackson. 'She doesn't know any of you because she only recently moved to the area. She lives on Kerrera.'

In the murmur of comments that followed, Merryn glanced round the room. There, to her surprise and delight was Emily Elizabeth Carmichael. Before she could stop herself, her excitement bubbled over.

'Emily,' she said. 'I know Emily.'

The girl who had been captured by Ammonia Begonia Clickfinger shook her head and looked puzzled.

'I don't know you,' she said. 'I'm sorry, but I've never seen you before.'

'I must be mistaken,' said Merryn, instantly regretting that she'd let her enthusiasm run away with her. 'I'm sorry. You must have a double.'

'Strange,' said Mrs Jackson, 'a double with the same name. That's unusual, but not impossible, I suppose. Anyway, Emily, perhaps you'd like to look after Merryn. Show her round and tell her everything she needs to know.'

Emily smiled. It was the same smile that had shone on Emily's face when Clickfinger's spells had started to unravel, but it was a smile that showed no sign of recognition. Merryn found it hard to understand. They'd shared such a mixture of terror and triumph that every detail was fixed in her own mind for ever. How could Emily have forgotten? Magic was the answer, of course, but it still seemed strange. Somehow, she had to persuade Emily to wear the crystal, but how could she do that when Emily didn't remember anything?

Meanwhile, in one of the first year classrooms, Hamish looked round apprehensively. It seemed huge after the village school he'd attended before moving to Scotland. He was worried about being the odd one out. He scanned the unfamiliar faces and then broke into a grin when he caught sight of Peter Watson.

Seeing Peter made a huge difference to the way he was feeling. Whatever else happened, he decided there and then that Peter would be his best friend. Then his grin faded as he remembered that Peter wouldn't recognise him. Still, he thought, we can get to know one another all over again. He hurried to grab the desk next to the one that Peter had chosen.

'Hi, he said, 'I'm Hamish and I don't know anyone at all.'

'I'm Peter,' came the reply. 'Neither do I.'

'Settle down,' said the teacher, 'and let's get to know one another. Starting at the back, stand in turn and say your name.'

Hamish tried to fit names to faces. He dreaded having to stand, having to call out his name, having everyone turn to stare at him. But fairly soon, it was over and the teacher continued.

'I'm Mr Cummins,' he said. 'I'm your English teacher as well as your form teacher and I have some exciting news. It's unusual to have a trip so early in the school year, but this half-term's work will be based on a real place. You're going to do different kinds of writing—directions, factual accounts, poetry and fiction. On Friday we're going to visit a castle. I expect you to arrive with a packed lunch, sensible footwear—boots or wellingtons, waterproofs and writing materials. I trust you can all supply those things, and if you have a camera that would be useful too. We're not going far, just across the bay to Kerrera.'

Hamish groaned and Mr Cummins pounced.

'Stand up Hamish McQueen,' he said. 'Why the groan?'

'Because I live there, Sir.'

'Then I shall expect your account to be perfect,' said Mr Cummins.

Hamish groaned again. 'I set myself up for that, didn't I?' He gave a rueful grin. 'But I don't have to come to school first, do I? Can't I meet you off the ferry?'

'If you're angling for an extra hour in bed you can forget it,' said Mr Cummins. 'I expect you here for registration as usual. Now, are there any questions?'

'Not a question,' said Jake who was sitting on the other side of Hamish. 'Only I've been before and I wondered if you knew that the castle is haunted.'

'There's nothing about that in the literature,' said Mr Cummins, 'and I don't believe in ghosts, although they can be effective in stories.'

Jake, close enough for Hamish to hear, mumbled under his breath. 'You'd believe it if you'd seen what I saw.'

Crumbs, thought Hamish, ghosts as well as witches, whatever next?

'Please sir, I only have school shoes and trainers,' said one of the girls.

There was a murmur of agreement from several others. It seemed that few of them possessed what Mr Cummins called sensible footwear.

'Then you'll have to manage with trainers,' said Mr Cummins, 'because we're going.'

At the end of their first day at High School Merryn and Hamish rushed to meet one another.

'You'll never believe this,' said Merryn.

At exactly the same moment, Hamish blurted out. 'You'll never believe this.' Then he stopped and grinned. 'You go first, I'll save the best until last.'

'Yours can't be better than mine,' said Merryn. 'It's Emily. She's in my class and she's been ever so kind to me.'

'Good one,' said Hamish. 'I can't beat it but I can match it. Guess who's in my class?' He didn't wait for an answer. 'It's Peter and he doesn't know anyone else because they've only just moved here. We've made friends already.'

His face broke into a huge grin. 'James is in school too. So mine's better than yours after all.'

'I guess you're right,' said Merryn. 'Isn't it brilliant. We've found the three most important ones. I wish Emily had remembered me, but of course she didn't.'

'Peter didn't know me either,' said Hamish, 'but I don't care. We can still be friends, and I nearly forgot, there's a boy called Jake. He says Gylen Castle is haunted. Do you think he's right?'

Merryn didn't answer. She was already deep in thought. She had to get Emily, James and Peter together. It would be easier than trying to talk to them separately. She had to persuade them to wear the crystal pendants, and that, especially for the boys, might prove difficult.

'I don't think we should rush into giving them the crystals,' she said. 'Let's make friends first. We don't want to scare them away.'

'I'm not sure,' said Hamish. 'We mustn't wait too long. I'm not happy about Twitch. I can't believe she'll stay away for ever. She said she'd pay me back for burning The Book of Spells. And if she turns up at school I'm not the only one who'll need protecting.'

The second day at school brought another welcome surprise. Who should walk into the classroom, but Rosie McRae. Hamish looked up with an excited smile. But it turned to a frown when he saw that Rosie, who looked far too small to be in High School, was clenching her fists and looking at the floor as if she was overcome with nerves.

'Rosie has come from Colonsay,' said Mr Cummins. 'She should have arrived yesterday but there was a problem with the plane so she had to come on the ferry. Now, who's going to look after her until she finds her way about?'

Hamish looked round. No one offered and Rosie looked as if she wanted to sink into the ground. He put up his hand and the room was filled with exclamations of surprise and a smattering of sniggers.

Someone called out, 'but you're a boy and she's a girl.'

'So what?' Hamish retorted. 'I have a sister. I'm used to girls. Besides we have something in common. We both live on islands.'

'Well,' said Mr Cummins, 'if it's fine with Rosie, it's fine with me.'

Rosie didn't look up. She didn't speak. All she managed was a nod of her head.

'So that's settled,' said Mr Cummins. 'Come on Jake, move to one of the empty desks and let Rosie sit next to Hamish.'

Jake muttered something inaudible as he gathered up his belongings, scraped back his chair and stomped to another desk. Rosie, still looking at the floor, came to sit next to Hamish. She gave him a quick sideways glance and mouthed her silent thanks.

At the desk on Hamish's other side, Peter frowned. From across the room, Jake scowled. Oh! crumbs, thought Hamish. All I wanted to do was be nice to Rosie. It looks as if Peter doesn't like girls and Jake's mad because he didn't want to move. Now what am I supposed to do? I don't see why we can't all be friends together.

Chapter 10

The day of the Kerrera trip arrived and Hamish grumbled all the way to the ferry.

'It's really silly having to trail all the way to school just so I can turn round and trail all the way back again.'

'Give it a rest,' said Merryn. 'You'll have a day out of school and you'll have time to talk to the others. See what you can find out about Peter and Rosie. We need to get to know them better and this is the perfect chance. Find out about Jake and his ghost too. That should be interesting.'

'I suppose so,' said Hamish, 'but I still think I could have had an extra hour in bed.'

In the Hostel where the island children lived during the week, Rosie woke early. She was far too excited to lie in bed. There was no turning over, no snuggling under the duvet to hide her eyes from the morning light. The thought of an island, however small was enough to put a smile on her face. She was island born, she loved her island home and one of her ambitions was to visit every other island in Scotland. She'd been to Mull, Iona, Islay and Jura. Kerrera was another one to tick off her list.

She leaned on her windowsill and looked out over the rooftops to the harbour. Cars and lorries were disappearing into a ferry, and she felt a pang—a sudden ache of longing deep down in her chest. She watched the ferry pull away from the pier. If it had been going to Colonsay she would have been tempted to run and catch it before it set out to sea, but there was no need because tonight she would be going home for the weekend.

She focused on Kerrera, on the boats at the end of the island nearest to Oban, but they weren't the reason for her excitement. From the Colonsay ferry she knew that the south end of Kerrera was almost deserted. She always dashed to the window to catch a glimpse of the castle perched high on a cliff above the sea. That was where they were heading today. Smiling to herself she dressed in jeans, T-shirt, fleece and wellingtons instead of the school uniform that she already hated. Then she packed her small rucksack with the things that Mr Cummins had listed.

An hour or so later, the class, with Mr Cummins and a student called Miss Turner, had left school, boarded the small ferry and were arriving on Kerrera. Rosie, totally unlike the shy girl who'd arrived in school three days earlier, was first to disembark. She looked round with shining eyes, eager to set out along the rough island track. Behind her she could hear some of the girls squealing and leaping between the puddles as they tried not to get their trainers dirty.

Words like 'boring' followed her up the brae, and she felt that she'd never get used to the other children. Hamish was the only one who'd been kind to her, but his friend Peter had been ignoring her and that made her feel uncomfortable. So she strode out on her own, splashing through puddles, eager to leave the sound of voices behind.

'Not so fast, Rosie.' Mr Cummins called. 'I need to say a few words before we go any further.'

Shuffling her feet impatiently she listened to the rules about staying close together and not wandering off. When they reached the castle, Mr Cummins said they must read the explanatory panels and make notes. Later they would have to write a factual account. For the weekend homework they could be more imaginative and write a story. That appealed to Rosie. She hadn't a clue what she'd write, but once she was inside the castle she'd let her imagination run wild.

As soon as Mr Cummins finished speaking, Rosie strode out again, way ahead of the others.

'Come on, Peter,' said Hamish, 'let's catch her up.'

'Why?' Peter asked. 'Maybe she wants to be on her own.'

'No,' said Hamish. 'I think she finds it hard to make friends. It must feel strange coming to a big school when you've spent all your life on a tiny island.'

'I suppose so,' said Peter, 'but she's a girl and I don't know much about girls. I just have brothers. I won't know what to say to her. Aren't girls a bit soppy?'

'Some of them are,' said Hamish, 'but my sister isn't. She's as brave as anything and...' He stopped himself from saying more about Merryn and he pointed up the track to where Rosie had paused to take a photograph.

'Look at Rosie. She may be little and pretty, but she's definitely not soppy.'

'OK,' said Peter, 'but I think we'd better ask if she wants us to join her.'

They jogged up the track, quickly covering the twenty metres that separated them from Rosie. As they reached her, she put her camera back in its case and gave a shy smile.

'We weren't sure if you'd want us to walk with you,' said Hamish.

Rosie shook her head. 'Company's fine.' She looked back down the track. 'As long as you're not frightened of getting your feet wet.'

The three of them walked on together, not too far ahead, and always in sight of Mr Cummins who was having to chivvy the others along. Farther back, Miss Turner, who seemed to be struggling for breath, was bringing up the rear.

They passed Horseshoe Bay and Hamish told them about the King's Field where Alexander II had died. He said that at one time, there were over a hundred galleys anchored in the bay and he pointed out the whitewashed cottages that had been built for slate quarry workers. Then they climbed to Upper Gylen farm where they paused until Mr Cummins joined them. As soon as he caught them up, they were off again, down the other side towards Lower Gylen. But before they reached The Tea Garden, Hamish turned onto a grassy track that led to the castle.

'Stop there,' Mr Cummins shouted. 'No-one goes near the castle until we're all together.'

Hamish sighed and leaned against the gate. 'We'll be here for ages,' he said. 'Tell us about Colonsay while we're waiting.'

Rosie nodded her head towards the group who were dawdling along the track. 'I expect some people, especially those back there would hate it, but I love it. It's the best place in the whole world. If you like being out of doors it's great, but if you want shops and swimming pools and cinemas it wouldn't do at all. I know every single person and every single person knows me. There were only eight of us in school and the next oldest to me was only nine. So I'm not used to having friends of my own age. It feels strange here. I miss my mum and dad and my little sister and I miss not being able to go out after school with my dog and my pony.'

'Sounds tough,' said Hamish, 'but what's the island like?'

'Brilliant,' she said. 'There are hills,' she pointed across to Mull, 'nothing like those of course. You can climb our highest one, Carnan Eoin, in half an hour, and then you look down on Kiloran Bay with its golden sands. There are woods too and the ones round Colonsay House have snowdrops in January and bluebells in June. The air smells good too, all flowers and bog myrtle and salty sea. The mainland smells of nothing but petrol fumes and chips.'

'Will you really come to school in a plane?' asked Peter.

'Yes, but it's just a tiny one. Sometimes I'll come on the ferry, but that takes two and a half hours. When my mum was at school there were only three ferries a week so she had to stay in the hostel for weeks at a time. Now, thank goodness, I can go home for weekends. I don't think I could stick it otherwise.'

Eventually, the rest of the class caught up and they all walked along the grassy track until the castle came into view. With sheer walls, crow-stepped gables and narrow window slits it towered above a cliff that dropped towards the sea. As they toiled up the steep hill they saw that the castle wasn't actually at the top.

For a while it dipped out of sight and then, as they crossed the rough grassland, it reappeared. Set in the side of the cliff, it had a wooden staircase leading down to an open doorway.

Hamish looked at Rosie and Peter. They were standing still, staring. Rosie's mouth was slightly open. Peter was frowning and scratching his head. Could it be that the sight of the castle had stirred a memory?

Chapter 11

'Now,' said Mr Cummins, 'you're safe as long as there's no pushing and shoving on the stairs. So we'll split into groups. Those who are outside can read the Information Boards, make notes, sketch the castle and have an early lunch.'

He looked at Hamish, Peter and Rosie. 'You three can go in first.'

'No thanks,' said Hamish. 'We'd rather go last. If the slow walkers go first they can set off back with Miss Turner. If we go in last, we'll soon catch up.'

'That's a good idea,' said Mr Cummins. 'Now, I won't give you a lecture. This is an exercise in finding and presenting information. You can write, draw, take photographs, anything as long as it's about the castle. You have three weeks to put it all into a little book. The results will give me a good idea of your capabilities. So don't let yourselves down. For this weekend's homework you can try fiction. Stories set in the castle are to be handed in first thing on Monday morning.'

Some of the groups were in and out of the castle in a few minutes. It was as if they couldn't find anything of interest. Others took their time. Hamish noticed that each time Jake came out he tagged onto the next group and went inside again and again.

'Did you see Jake?' he asked Peter. 'I bet he's looking for the ghost. Do you think he really saw one?'

'I don't know,' said Peter, 'but I'd like to know what he thinks he saw.'

After lunch, and after Rosie had taken lots of photos of the outside of the castle, their turn came. Mr Cummins sat on the steps, and Jake joined their small group. Everyone else left with Miss Turner.

Jake was already inside when Hamish went down the steps into the stone-lined passageway. Rosie, close behind him, stopped so abruptly on the threshold that Peter bumped into her. She staggered and leaned against the wall.

'I'm sorry,' said Peter. 'I wasn't expecting you to stop. Did I hurt you?'

'No.' Rosie wiped her eyes. 'You gave me a shock that's all, but I feel ever so strange. It's as if I've come through that door before—but I can't have.'

Jake, who had turned to listen, nodded as if he understood. 'I told you this place is haunted. At least it was last time I came. I definitely saw a ghost, but I've looked everywhere today and I can't find her.'

Peter stepped out through the doorway and then came back inside. He opened his mouth to speak, but he stopped as if he didn't know what to say. He looked at Rosie and his words all came out in a rush.

'I know what you mean, and you're right. It is odd because I've never been before and yet I feel as if I have. Only it wasn't like this inside. I must be mixing it up with another castle.'

'Well, I'm not,' said Rosie. 'I've never been in a castle in my life.'

'Don't worry about it,' said Jake. 'You're supersensitive like me. I feel things that other people can't feel, and I see things that other people can't see. No one believes me, but it's true. It's a sort of sixth sense. Some people call it second sight. Maybe you have it too.'

Hamish watched them all, aware of what was happening, but afraid of saying something he'd regret. Stepping over the threshold had stirred memories. He pressed his lips together to stop himself from blurting out the truth. He wished Merryn was there to tell him what to say.

Once they were inside, the strange feelings that Rosie and Peter had experienced seemed to fade away. They looked round together, discussing the information on the panels, making notes and trying to imagine what it was like in 1647 when the castle was looted and burned.

Rosie leaned on the upstairs windowsill. 'Look,' she said. 'There's Colonsay.' She stood aside while the boys took turns to peer at the faint shape on the horizon.

'It doesn't look much from here,' said Hamish.

Rosie laughed. 'I know,' she said. 'It's impossible to imagine beaches and seabird cliffs and lochs and hills and woods. It doesn't look big enough to hold them all, but it is. You'll have to come and visit and then I can show you round.'

'I'd love that,' said Hamish.

'Come on,' came a shout from outside the castle. 'It's time to head back.'

Hamish looked out of the other window and waved at Mr Cummins. 'Two minutes,' he called. 'We've almost finished.'

He turned to Jake. 'Before we go I want to know about your ghost. When did you see it and exactly where was it?'

'I'll be putting it in my story,' said Jake, 'but I suppose I can tell you. We were on a trip. It was the last week of term, before I left Primary School.'

He ran down the stairs, stood in the passageway and stopped a few paces from the door. 'She was here, looking at me and saying something. I couldn't hear the words, but she looked frantic. I'm sure she was asking for help.'

Rosie shivered. 'That gives me goose-bumps,' she said, 'but I'd still like to know what she looked like.'

'Like a shadow,' said Jake. 'No, not a shadow, shadows are dark and she was sort of see-through. I told her I could see her and I tried to touch her. In fact I waved my hand right through her. That was spooky so I stopped. When we left she tried to follow me. The last time I saw her she was trying to get out through the doorway.' He shrugged. 'But for some reason she couldn't.'

Hamish was desperate to know more. He didn't want to sound too eager in case Jake started to ask awkward questions. He must have seen one of the captive girls, but which one? Apparently there had been lots of them, but the only ones he knew were Emily, Rosie, Lisa, Heather and Hazel.

'Was she an old ghost?' he asked. 'I mean, was she an old woman wearing old-fashioned clothes?'

'No.' Jake screwed up his eyes as he tried to picture what he'd seen. 'She was just a girl, taller than me, with lots of dark curly hair.'

Emily! The name flew into Hamish's head. To his relief he managed not to blurt it out.

'What was she wearing?' Rosie asked.

'A cardigan, it looked too big for her, but, hang on a minute.' He screwed up his eyes again. 'It was hazy because I could see the wall through it, but it had coloured patterns all over it.'

'Flowers,' said Hamish. He knew he'd spoken too quickly because Jake's head gave a sudden jerk. 'I mean, could it have been flowers?'

'It was flowers.' Jake looked suspiciously at Hamish. 'How did you know? You're hiding something. Come on, I've told you my story. Now I want to know yours.'

'It was just a guess,' Hamish bluffed. 'After all, flowers are a popular pattern. Come on, we'd better go before Mr Cummins calls again.'

The journey back passed without a hitch, until, as they neared the school, Miss Turner fell into step beside Hamish.

'I believe you live on Kerrera,' she said. 'I expect you know everyone who lives on the island.'

Hamish stammered as a sudden tremor fluttered at his throat. 'No, not... not really,' He reached up to lay his hand over his crystal pendant. It was vibrating. He took a deep breath before he spoke again. 'We only moved there a few weeks ago, and it's not for long, just until mum and dad find a house to buy.'

'And where will that be?'

'No idea,' said Hamish, 'not far away because they don't want us to change schools again.'

Miss Turner nodded. 'No, that would be disruptive, especially for your sister.'

There was something menacing in the way she said 'sister'. The crystal vibrated more strongly. Thoughts raced around inside his head. She's a witch and she knows about Merryn. Before he could move away she reached out to grab him, but she must have felt the power of his crystal and hag-stone because her hand drew back quickly.

'Before that, you were on Tiree weren't you,' she insisted. 'I had a friend there, but she disappeared. I think you must have known her.'

'How could I know her if she'd disappeared,' he said. 'And now I'd better get back before Mr Cummins misses me.'

He squeezed his way through the children and ran until he reached the relative safety of the boys' toilets. There, with his hand on the amethyst pendant he sent an urgent message to Tobias.

Chapter 12

Miss Turner stamped her foot and scowled as Hamish slipped out of sight. She'd felt something even more powerful than a hag-stone. It told her that Merryn MacQueen wasn't the only one with magical powers. Her brother possessed something unusual too. Determined to find out what it was, she strode into the classroom where the pupils were discussing their trip to Gylen Castle.

Hamish looked up. His eyes met hers. He lifted his chin defiantly and forced himself not to blink. He was daring her to try touching him again. He kept on staring, until, defeated, she turned and stormed out of the classroom.

It was useless trying to get information out of him. She was still furious with him for burning The Book of Spells, and she would never forget the part he'd played in stopping her from winning The Clickfinger Locket. She wouldn't let a mere boy get the better of her, but she needed help, an ally—someone to spy on him.

Peter was her first choice, but he and Hamish were already friends. Jake? Yes, there was something strange about Jake. He'd spent most of their time at Gylen going in and out of the castle as if he was looking for something. Perhaps he too had been looking for The Book of Spells. She'd get to know him. She'd discover his fears and his worries, and she'd use them to blackmail him.

Unaware that Miss Turner had followed him home, Jake ran up to his bedroom. He changed out of his school uniform, whistled to Rex and set off for a walk. Going back to Gylen Castle had unsettled him. It had reminded him of the ghost he'd tried to forget. He'd seen ghosts before and they hadn't bothered him. This one had been different. He hadn't heard her voice, although she'd tried to speak to him. He was sure she'd been begging for help, and he'd had to leave her, trapped in the castle, lost in the past. He couldn't forget the desperate look in her eyes. Now, all he wanted was to play with Rex and chase the memory out of his mind.

For several minutes the game went well. Rex bounded after the ball, dropped it at Jake's feet, and panted eagerly as he waited for it to be thrown again. Thinking to make the task a little harder, Jake threw the ball into the undergrowth. Rex chased after it, then barked several times before scurrying back with his tail between his legs.

'Where's the ball?' asked Jake. 'Go on, Rex, find it.'

He walked towards the bushes, but Rex hung back, whimpered, sat down and refused to move.

'What's wrong?' He took hold of Rex's collar and tried to pull him along, but the dog wouldn't budge. 'Well I don't want to lose your ball,' he said. 'You can stay there, but I'm going to look for it.'

He moved towards the bushes and there stood Miss Turner, her arm held high, the ball clenched in her fist.

'Is this what you're looking for?' she called.

'Yes, thanks,' Jake called back. 'There's no need to come across the grass. Just throw it.'

But Miss Turner was already on her way. As she came closer, Rex stood up and backed away with a low growl rumbling in his throat.

'That dog's a menace,' said Miss Turner. 'He tried to attack me, back there in the bushes. He needs locking up. I've a good mind to report him to the police.'

Jake put a protective hand on Rex's head. 'Please don't,' he gasped. 'He's never growled at anyone before. Something must have frightened him. He's usually a big softie.'

'I don't believe you,' said Miss Turner. 'Once a bad dog always a bad dog. I don't trust him.'

She pointed a finger at Rex and his growl grew louder. His lips curled. He bared his teeth and took a step towards Miss Turner. Jake had no idea what happened next. One second Rex looked as if he was about to spring at Miss Turner, the next second he was lying on the grass, his mouth open, his tongue lolling out as if he was dead.

Jake dropped to his knees and cradled the dog's head. 'Wake up,' he begged. 'What's wrong with you?'

'It's what he deserved,' said Miss Turner.

'What have you done to him?' Jake demanded. 'You did something to make him angry. Then you...you killed him.'

Miss Turner laughed. 'Not yet,' she said. 'He's not dead, just stunned. He'll be fine as long as you do everything you're told.'

Jake struggled to hold back his tears. He sniffed and looked up at Miss Turner. 'And if...if I don't?' he stammered. 'What then?'

'The end of Rex,' she said with a laugh. 'The choice is yours. Are you going to do as you're told, or are you going to say goodbye to your precious pet?'

Jake could barely find his voice. 'That's not a choice,' he gasped. 'You know I'll do anything to save him.'

'That's all right then,' she said with a smirk, 'and don't worry. It's nothing very terrible. I'm not asking you to murder anyone. Think of it as a game. I'm the Spy Mistress and you're my Chief Assistant. All you have to do is keep an eye on Hamish MacQueen and his sister Merryn.'

'But I don't know Merryn.'

'You will, soon enough,' she said, 'and there'll be others too. Find out about their friends. Watch them. Tell me everything they do, everything they say and about everyone they meet.'

Jake's eyes filled with tears as he fondled Rex's ears. He'd been a puppy on Jake's sixth birthday. Now he was six and Jake was twelve and life without him would be unbearable. He knew that Miss Turner was asking him to do something wrong, but what could he do? He hated the thought of spying, but he couldn't risk losing Rex. Miss Turner was leaving him without a choice. Watching Hamish and his friend Peter didn't seem too huge a task as they were in the same class. Merryn and her friends would be more difficult, but hopefully not impossible.

'All right,' he said with a sniff. 'I don't like it, but I'll do it if you make Rex better and promise not to hurt him again.'

Miss Turner's eyes narrowed and she took a step closer. 'Don't think you can bargain with me,' she snapped. 'I'll make Rex better when I'm good and ready. Oh! I almost forgot. There's just one more teeny, weeny little thing. You're not going to like this either, but it can't be helped. There's a girl called Emily Carmichael. I want something that belongs to her. I don't mind what it is. It doesn't have to be valuable, a pencil, a shoelace, one of her notebooks, even a button from her coat will do.'

'But that's stealing,' Jake protested.

'Stealing or not,' she said, 'you'll do it because you don't want to say goodbye to Rex. Now that's settled I expect a full report. There's no need to look for me. I'll find you wherever you are and don't be surprised if I look different. Sometimes a disguise is necessary, but if we have a password I can let you know it's me. How about 'Goodbye Rex'?' She laughed. 'That should keep you on your toes.'

Jake shuddered. Only a really mean person could have thought of such a password. It was horrible, and this weird woman thought it was funny. He wanted to tell her to go away, to do her own spying and stealing, but it was too risky. Watching and listening wouldn't be too difficult, but stealing was another matter. It didn't matter if it was valuable or worthless. Stealing was wrong. Deep down inside he guessed that Emily Carmichael was in danger, but how could he choose between his dog and a girl he didn't even know.

'I'll do it,' he said, 'even though I know it's wrong, but please, please wake Rex up.'

Whatever Miss Turner did, it was done so quickly that Jake hadn't a clue how it happened. Rex gave an enormous yawn, stood up and picked up his ball. Overwhelmed with relief, Jake stood up too. He looked round, but Miss Turner was no-where to be seen.

Hamish could hardly wait to tell Merryn that the woman who was supposed to be a student teacher, wasn't a student teacher at all.

'She tried to grab me,' he said, 'and when she couldn't she was as mad as could be. My crystal vibrated so I knew she was a witch. She wanted to know all about you and Tiree and Kerrera and Gylen Castle. She said she had a friend who'd disappeared on Tiree. She was trying to trick me into telling her what happened. I didn't tell her anything. I ran away and called Tobias. He asked lots of questions, but he didn't seem to know who she was. He'll try his best, but he might need more information before he can get rid of her.'

Merryn shook her head in dismay. Things were happening too quickly. The appearance of another witch was worrying, especially as they knew nothing at all about her. She would have to put her faith in Tobias, and hope that Miss Turner, whoever she was, would leave Hamish alone.

Chapter 13

Hamish couldn't enjoy the weekend. He worried about seeing Miss Turner again and he was struggling with his homework. He found it hard to invent a story about the castle when his head was full of things that had really happened. He wanted to write the truth. It was strange enough to be fiction, but Merryn wouldn't let him.

'No,' she said, 'you mustn't. If other witches hear it they'll know we were involved. We have to keep it secret.'

In the end he wrote about pirates hiding treasure in the castle, but he knew it wasn't very good. He handed it in on Monday morning, but all his thoughts went out of his head when Mr Cummins said that Miss Turner had met with an accident and was unable to come to school.

He covered his face to hide the grin that stretched from one ear to the other. It was a relief to concentrate on schoolwork without Miss Turner watching his every move.

On Tuesday morning, Mr Cummins arrived with a pile of exercise books. 'There's little to commend in these,' he said as he handed them round. 'I told you to use your imaginations and what do you give me? Echoes of things you've read or seen on TV. Out of all those efforts there are only two with any originality. Jake's ghost story is good, but this one is even better.'

He dropped a book on Peter's desk. 'Tell me how you came up with the idea.'

Peter looked down in embarrassment. 'I don't know,' he mumbled. 'It just came into my head.'

'If that's true,' said Mr Cummins, 'we have a genius in our midst. Mind you, imagination isn't everything. Your handwriting is atrocious and your spelling and punctuation leave a lot to be desired. However, the story is highly original so come to the front and read it aloud.'

Peter shook his head. 'I'd rather not. Can't you read it, please?'

'Your story, your voice,' said Mr Cummins. 'Come on. Read!'

Reluctantly, Peter picked up his book. He stood in front of the class and coughed self-consciously. Somehow, after struggling with the first sentence he was carried along with the excitement of the story.

'I couldnt believe it at first. I thought I was dreaming but then it turned into a nightmare and after that it wasnt a dream or a nightmare. It was real. I was in a car with a mad old woman. We were flying through clouds and then we landed in front of Gylen Castle. Then this mad old woman made me count to seven and we jumped over the doorstep. And we werent in the castle at all. We were inside a room that didnt have doors or windows. She told me to cleer the table and do the washing up. There were dirty stinky pots everywhere. I stacked them on a tray and started to carry them to the sink. Then this cat appeared but it wasnt a normal cat. It was huge and its name was Spitfire. It was easy to see why because it started spiting round my ancles and it got under my feet and triped me up. All the pots went flying and the

woman went mad. She screamed and then she changed into a hidious old witch with warts all over her face and a horrible black finger with a nail like a dragons claw. Then she said I was useless and she clicked her horrible finger and I started to feel really wierd. I knew I was shrinking, but that wasn't all. My arms and legs disappeared and my body turned black and the next thing I knew I'd turned into a slug.'

There were gasps of horror and titters of laughter. Mr Cummins glared and shouted at everyone to be quiet. Hamish was bewildered. Peter wasn't supposed to remember, and what about Rosie? He turned to look at her. She was clutching the desk so tightly that her knuckles were white. Her head was bent so he couldn't see her face, but he heard her sniff. He wanted to reassure her, but before he could say anything, Peter was persuaded to carry on reading.

'Then she picked me up and put me in a cage with some moldy old cabbage leaves and...'

The pause had unsettled him. 'I'm sorry,' he said. 'I can't read any more. It's too horrible.'

'Nonsense,' said Mr Cummins. 'It's only a story.'

Hamish bit his lip to stop himself blurting out that every word was true. Rosie stifled a sob and pushed her fingers in her ears.

One of the boys called out. 'Go on. We want to know what happened next.'

There were murmurs of agreement from the rest of the class, so Peter took a deep breath and carried on.

'The cage was in a smelly room with lots of other cages and the witch left me there. I was traped and couldnt do anything except stay there and eat cabbage leaves. I knew I wasnt the only one in a cage because every time the witch came into the room there was lots of rusling and squeeking as if everyone was hiding. She didnt come very often just to bring more cabbage leaves and I don't want to eat cabbage again for as long as I live. I don't know how long I was there but it seemed like years. Then one day she took me out of the cage and put me in a box and my brother James opened it and when he saw me he gasped and said that's what had hapened to him and he couldn't bare to tuch me. I wanted to shout and scream and tell him that it was me but I couldn't because I was a slug. So a girl picked me up and the witch sprayed some green stuff all over me and it covered me in green bubbles and I started to grow. Then there was a flash and a bang and an exploshun with lots of green smoke and I wasnt a slug any more and my brother was hugging me and saying he was glad it was me and we were laughing and crying all at the same time and I wasn't a slug any more and that's all I can remember.*

When he came to the last word he closed the book, scurried back to his seat and hid his face in his hands.

'Any comments?' Mr Cummins asked.

'It's brilliant,' said Hamish, 'because it's true.' Hastily he corrected himself. 'I mean it sounds true. Even though it's magic and impossible, it makes you believe it's true.'

'Exactly,' said Mr Cummins, 'and which particular bits made it believable? Hands up, let's hear from someone else.'

'It was the laughing and crying,' said one of the girls.

'The cabbage leaves,' said another, 'the bit about never wanting to eat cabbage again.'

'It was the last few words,' said a boy. 'When he said that's all I can remember it made it sound as if it really happened.'

'All right Peter, you can come out of hiding,' said Mr Cummins. 'Everyone thought your story was excellent so there's no need to be bashful. The idea was brilliant, but a careful edit will make it even better. With your permission I'm going to print it out. Homework for everyone will be to rewrite it with correct spelling, punctuation and best handwriting. Now, off you go for lunch.'

Everyone else left in a hurry, but Rosie didn't move for ages. Hamish and Peter waited for her and they went to the dining hall together. They sat down with their food, but after one mouthful Peter put his knife and fork down.

'When we went into the castle,' he said, 'all those weird ideas came into my head. I didn't have to think about my story at all. It just poured out as if it was true.' He shuddered. 'Why would I imagine myself as a horrible, black, slimy slug? '

'Because it's...' Hamish stopped himself. He needed to talk to Merryn before he told the truth. 'It's like a dream. The oddest things happen in dreams. I once dreamed I was being eaten by a crocodile. I can remember it as if it was real. I think I'd rather be a slug.'

'You wouldn't if you'd been one,' said Peter. 'I mean if you'd imagined being one, like I did.'

'Or a mouse,' Rosie broke her silence with a whisper. She pulled a crumpled paper out of her bag and handed it to Hamish. 'It's the story that I wrote for homework,' she said, 'only it was so scary that I screwed it up and wrote a different one instead.'

She sat, twisting her fingers and watching anxiously as Hamish and Peter read it together.

Peter's eyes opened wider and wider as he read the words. 'I don't understand,' he said. 'How could we both write the same thing? How could we both invent a cat called Spitfire? And I'd forgotten the witch's name, but Rosie's right. It was Clickfinger. It really was.'

Hamish nodded. 'Ammonia Begonia Clickfinger,' he said. 'Something similar happened to me too.'

Chapter 14

Hamish was bursting to tell Merryn all that had happened, but he forced himself to wait until they were behind the closed door of his bedroom. After all, witches were everywhere and one of them might be listening. Inside the cottage with its protection of hag-stones, sitting next to Merryn with her sea-bean and hag-stone necklace was the safest place he knew. Here, he felt able to take out the photocopy of Peter's story.

'What do you think of this?' he asked. 'I have to correct it for homework. Everyone in the class got a copy.'

Merryn read in silence, and when she came to the end she dropped the paper as if it had burned her fingers.

'You'll have to explain to Peter,' she said, 'and that means telling James and Emily too.'

'And Rosie,' said Hamish. 'Her story was more or less the same. She even mentioned Clickfinger. I said something similar had happened to me.'

'I wish you hadn't,' said Merryn.

'So do I,' said Hamish,' but it just came out. I'm sorry.'

Merryn had wanted to make friends with the other children before she explained about the witches, but events had taken over. The trip to the castle had made two of them remember. Somehow they all had to be told.

'We've got to get them together,' she said, 'but not in school in case we're overheard. If there's one witch around there might be others. We'll have to be careful.

I wonder if they could come here on Saturday. I think mum and dad would be pleased. They were hoping we'd make friends.'

'Great idea, only we can't ask Rosie,' said Hamish. 'She goes home to Colonsay at weekends. I bet she'll mention it again though, and if she does, I'll have to tell her something.'

'Don't,' said Merryn. 'Not until we've spoken to the others. They need to understand what happened before we give them the hag-stones and crystals.

For Merryn and Hamish the rest of the week passed without incident. They got used to going to school by way of the ferry. Rosie seemed to be settling down to life on the mainland too.

'I'd rather be on Colonsay,' she said, 'but there's one good thing about being here.' She grinned at Hamish and Peter. 'It's the first time I've had friends of my own age.'

A sudden shadow crossed her face. 'I'm just worried about our castle stories. I don't understand how we could both imagine the same thing.'

'Coincidence,' said Peter. 'It must be. There's no other explanation.'

'Keep your voice down,' Hamish whispered. 'Or maybe Jake's right. Maybe something happened in the past and we sensed it.'

Rosie covered her mouth and whispered back. 'If it was a memory it must have happened, like the MacDougall's fleeing for their lives. But this was a witch and witches aren't real. They're just in fairy stories.'

'Well, I'm trying to forget it,' said Peter, 'and I think you should too.'

'Forget what?' asked Jake as he sneaked up behind them.

Peter's quick wits provided an answer. 'That silly story I wrote,' he said. 'It gave Rosie a nightmare. I wish I'd never written it.'

Their parents had arranged for Emily, James and Peter to spend Saturday on Kerrera. Merryn and Hamish, waiting on the slipway to meet them, watched as they boarded the ferry on the far side of the narrow strip of water. A few minutes later all five of them were walking up the brae on their way to Gylen Castle.

James, who hadn't spoken to the girls before, seemed shy at first, but he soon started to ask questions about the island. Peter and Hamish, who were already the best of friends, strode on ahead. When they were out of earshot of the other three, Peter stopped.

'Look here,' he said, 'I'm not stupid. Tell me what's going on. You haven't just invited us for a picnic. There's something else, and whatever it is, I don't like it. Rosie should be here too, shouldn't she?'

Hamish nodded. 'There should be ten of you altogether, but we haven't found the other six. We weren't going to say anything until we'd found you all, but you wrecked our plans.'

Peter was indignant. 'What do you mean? How could I wreck your plans when I didn't know what they were?'

'Your story,' said Hamish, 'you spilled the beans, that's how. Sorry. It's not your fault. If Mr Cummins hadn't taken us to the castle you wouldn't have remembered.'

'Remembered!' Peter exclaimed. 'What do you mean, remembered? Don't tell me all the things I wrote are true.'

'Afraid so,' said Hamish.

Peter sat down with a bump, right there in the middle of the track. He put his head in his hands and made a terrible wailing sound. Hamish glanced at the others. They'd seen him fall and were running to see what was wrong.

Hamish knelt down and spoke urgently. 'Don't tell them anything. They'll find out soon enough.'

He pulled Peter to his feet. 'And don't worry. We've brought you here to tell you what really happened.' He turned and shouted to the others. 'It's OK. He's fine. He just needs to look where he's going.'

He hurried Peter along, refusing to answer his string of anxious questions.   'Merryn will explain,' he said. 'So you'll have to wait. Now stop talking and hurry up. I want to get to the castle before the others. I need to see what James and Emily do when they step inside.'

A little while later, Hamish ran down the wooden staircase into the castle, but he had to coax Peter to follow. 'If you want to know the rest you'll have to come in,' he said. 'They're nearly here, so for goodness sake get a move on.'

James appeared at the top of the steps and looked up at the castle. 'Brilliant,' he said, 'I've always liked castles.' He came down the steps, strode over the threshold and gave an involuntary shudder. 'I'm not sure about this one though. It's sort of... menacing.'

Emily was quiet until she reached the main room at the top of the stairs. There, she gave a frightened yelp, staggered and almost fell. She put her hand against the wall to steady herself as she lapsed into a strange kind of trance.

'I've been here before,' she whispered. 'There was a storm. It rained. I got soaked. I couldn't move. There was a mad old woman and she said...she said that I had to live here.' She snapped out of the trance, looked round wildly and wailed, 'I want my mum.'

'Hush.' Merryn folded her arms round Emily. 'It's OK. It's over. Come on, let's sit in the sun and I'll tell you all about it.'

Merryn went back to the very beginning. She talked about The Gift and the necklace of sea-beans and hag-stones; and of how they'd found the horse that cried at midnight. She spoke of the challenges they'd faced, of Roane The Selkie and The Fairy Folk. She explained how they'd eliminated the witch of Tiree and how they'd rescued the horse and discovered that he was really a young wizard.

'Then,' she said, 'we moved to Kerrera and this is where you three come into the story.'

She took two sheets of paper out of her rucksack. One was a photocopy of Peter's homework. The other was the page that Rosie had scrumpled up. She read the two stories aloud and from time to time she looked up to see how James and Emily were reacting. The emotions that crossed their faces changed from moment to moment. They registered amazement, fear, horror and disbelief. But finally they accepted the truth.

'It really happened,' said Emily. 'I don't want to believe it, but it's true. I know it is.'

'So do I,' said James,' but I can't remember how it ended.'

'We came to rescue you,' said Merryn, 'but before that, you three were amazing. Emily, you took Spitfire's collar off because he was choking...'

'and he turned into a wizard,' said Emily, 'and we rescued some other children. Now I remember.'

'And Clickfinger went to a competition,' added James. 'She made a mess of her spells and this woman...'

'The Grand High Witch,' Hamish prompted.

James nodded. 'Whoever she was, she waved a wand, only it was more like a snake.'

'It was a snake,' said Hamish. 'It was The Snake Wand and it got rid of Clickfinger.'

'And we all sang *Ding dong the witch is dead*,' said Peter.

'Not all,' said Emily with a sniff. 'Just the boys.'

Hamish glared at her. 'We had to celebrate somehow,' he said. 'After that, Clickfinger's spells unravelled and you all went home.'

'But why did we forget?' asked Peter.

'Because Clickfinger didn't want people to know,' said Merryn. 'She blocked it out of your minds. Imagine what a fuss there'd be if a story like that got into the newspapers.'

James raised his hand. 'Hush,' he said. 'I think someone's coming.'

Chapter 15

Someone was whistling. Five faces turned to the brow of the hill to see who it was. A dog ran towards them and close behind it came a fair-haired boy.

'It's Jake,' said Peter. 'What's he doing here?'

'Is that the boy who thought he saw a ghost?' asked Merryn.

'Yes,' said Hamish. 'He's got second sight or something weird. I don't trust him. He's a snooper. He's always turning up when we don't expect him.'

'I thought I'd find you here,' said Jake. 'I don't know what's go...' He stopped in shock and pointed at Emily.

'That's her. That's my ghost. I don't know what you're up to, but it's something fishy and I want to know what it is.'

'It's complicated,' said Merryn, 'and it only concerns those of us who were in the castle.'

'That includes me, then,' said Jake. 'I was in the castle when I saw her. She spoke to me. I tried to touch her but my hand went right through her. Ask her. She'll tell you it's true.'

Emily nodded. 'It is true,' she said. 'I remember his fair hair and his red jumper. I was desperate to go with him, but he went through the wall as if it wasn't there. I couldn't follow. I told Clickfinger that he'd seen me. She said she didn't want his sort sniffing out her secrets. She said he'd just think he'd seen a ghost.'

Jake scratched his head. 'That's what I did think, but I didn't go through a wall. I went out the way I went in, through the doorway. And who on earth is Clickfinger?

'A witch,' said Peter.

James had reached out to cover Peter's mouth, but he was too late.

'A witch,' Jake echoed. 'You're pulling my leg.' But even as he spoke he knew it was true. He also knew that Clickfinger wasn't the only witch. Miss Turner was a witch too.

Merryn looked at Jake. He was obviously involved, and now he knew about Clickfinger he might as well know the truth. On the other hand, she wasn't sure he could be trusted. The necklace lay still and silent round her neck. The crystal pendulum wasn't vibrating. There didn't seem to be any immediate danger, but a wave of uneasiness made her hesitate.

'You'd better tell me everything,' said Jake. 'Count me in and I won't tell anyone else.'

'And if we don't?' Merryn asked.

Jake shrugged. 'I don't know. I might be tempted to tell. It's a good story.'

'That's blackmail,' Hamish yelled.

'If you say so,' said Jake.

'We need to know more,' said Merryn. 'What else did you see?'

'Stone walls and steps,' said Jake. He pointed at Emily and added, 'nothing unusual except for her.'

'And you didn't see anyone else?'

'No,' said Jake. 'I'm always seeing ghosts so I didn't think much about it at first, but it was scary when she tried to speak to me. I'm sorry. I won't tell. It was a stupid thing to say. People think I'm odd enough as it is. It's just frustrating knowing half a story and being on the edge of something exciting.'

They all started to answer at once, but Merryn's indignant voice rose above the rest. 'Exciting! It's not some sort of jolly picnic. It's terrifying. There are Malevolent Witches all over the place and they know we're helping The Benevolent Wizards. So we're in danger. Every single one of us.'

She looked round at the others. They were staring at her in silence. James put a protective arm around Peter. Emily started chewing her nails.

'I'm sorry,' said Merryn. 'I didn't mean to spill it out like that. I'd planned what I was going to say and then you,' she glared at Jake, 'you messed it up. But now I've said it, I can't take it back, and anyway, it's true.'

Jake choked back his tears. He wanted to be friends with these five children. He didn't want to be Miss Turner's spy, but she'd threatened to kill Rex and he knew that she meant it.

'I'm sorry I came,' he mumbled unhappily. 'I think I've got more than I bargained for.'

'Yes, you have,' said Hamish, 'and it serves you jolly well right for butting in.' His hand went up to clutch his crystal and he wished that Tobias could be there to explain everything properly. Merryn was doing her best, but by the looks on all their faces she was making a mess of it.

'Don't worry,' he said, 'witches are a bit stupid. We've outwitted two of them and I don't think we'll see Miss Turner again.'

'Miss Turner was a witch?' Peter exclaimed.

Hamish nodded and slapped the flat of his hand against his forehead. 'Turner! I should have guessed.

It's a dead give away for a woman who can turn herself into someone else.'

Emily clutched Merryn's hand. 'What are we going to do?'

'We're going to work out a strategy. We'll…'

Before she could say anything else, a voice came out of the sunlit air.

'It's Tobias,' she said, and as the wizard appeared she ran into his arms. 'I'm so glad you're here, but how did you know I needed you?'

Tobias tousled Hamish's hair. 'A wish of your brother's alerted me to the fact, so here I am.' He held out his hands to Emily, James and Peter. 'You knew me as Spitfire and it is good to see you in your own world. But who is this?' He looked down at Jake. 'You were not involved with Clickfinger. Why are you here?'

Jake couldn't answer. He was struggling to recover from the sudden appearance of the bearded stranger.

'He's Jake,' said Hamish. 'He can see ghosts. He saw Emily when she was trapped in the castle. He's just turned up and he recognised her as soon as he saw her.'

'Interesting,' said Tobias. 'What else can you see? Tell me, Jake, what do I look like to you?'

'A bit odd,' said Jake. 'Not many men have such long hair, or such long beards.'

'Half close your eyes and look again,' said Tobias.

Looking more bewildered than ever, Jake did as he was told. He screwed up his eyelids and peered through his lashes. 'You look different,' he stammered. 'Your clothes are like something out of a history book or one of those films about Robin Hood.'

Tobias spoke in a gentle voice. 'Describe them to me,' he said. 'Tell me everything, down to the smallest detail. Start with my shoes.'

'Leather,' said Jake, 'dark red, sort of plum-coloured, with curled up toes and a seam down the middle. Tight trousers and a shirt in the same colour and a leather sporran on a belt.'

He rubbed his eyes and looked round at the others. They were standing in silence, wide-eyed, wondering what was going to happen next. To Merryn and Hamish, Jake's description was accurate. To the others it was a description of the wizard they'd known inside Clickfinger's fortress. Now, in the real world, all they could see was a tall, bearded man in grey trousers, walking boots and a black fleece.

'Anything else?' Tobias asked. 'Can you see patterns?'

'Gold on the shirt, all the way round the edge, in squiggles, a bit like those Celtic patterns that go round and round and never stop.' He stepped closer. 'It's on the sporran as well.'

Merryn's eyes filled with tears. Suddenly and miraculously she no longer felt alone. She sniffed and smiled up at Tobias. 'He has it too, hasn't he?'

'One more test, just to make sure,' said Tobias. He put his hands on Jake's shoulders and turned him round to face Merryn. She knew what to do. She lifted the necklace and the amethyst pendulum from inside her shirt and she clenched her fists in eager anticipation.

'Now, tell me what you see around her neck,' said Tobias.

Emily, James and Peter shrugged and shook their heads as if the question was really stupid. As far as they could see, there was nothing round Merryn's neck. Hamish, on the other hand, was hopping up and down in excitement. He was beginning to understand that there was more to Jake than an ability to see ghosts.

Jake shielded his eyes and turned his head away. 'Whatever it is, it's dazzling me. It's bright and it's sending out rays of light.'

'Colour?' asked Tobias.

'Purple,' said Jake, 'definitely purple, and hang on, there's something else. It's a strange sort of necklace.' He moved towards Merryn and peered more closely. 'It's made of stones and big flat beans.'

He turned to Tobias with a look of complete bewilderment on his face. 'What does it mean?' he asked.

'It means that you were born for a purpose,' said Tobias.

His face wreathed in smiles. He knelt on the grass, put his arms round Jake and beckoned Merryn to join them.

'This is a great day,' he said. 'Merryn, you are no longer the only one. Jake has The Gift too.'

Chapter 16

Tobias held out his hand and Hamish knew, without words, that he was asking for the bag of crystals and hag-stones. He handed it over and the wizard opened it and held up three amethyst pendants on silver chains. He gave one each to James. Peter and Emily.

'They're exactly like mine,' said Hamish, 'and you must never ever take them off. Don't worry about wearing them. Once they're round your necks they'll be invisible.

'But what do they do?' asked Peter.

'They should protect you,' said Tobias. 'As long as you wear them, witches will be unable to touch you. If a witch comes near you, the crystals will vibrate. If that happens you must contact me by placing your hand over the crystal and thinking of my name.'

'But why did you say should?' asked Emily.

'Ah! You saw the flaw,' said Tobias. 'I could not say that they will always protect you. They will struggle if you meet more than one witch at a time. And they are no barrier to The Snake Wand and The Grand High Witch. Where she is concerned, we are all at her mercy.'

'They're not much help then,' said James.

'They will protect you from all other witches,' said Tobias. 'But, as added protection I want you to keep a hag-stone with you at all times. Put your hand in the bag and one of the stones will choose you. As for The Grand High Witch, she rarely ventures out so we must hope that you never meet her.'

When Emily, James and Peter slipped the silver chains over their necks, they saw that the crystals were indeed invisible. When they put their hands in the bag, a hag-stone chose them. Jake got his hag-stone too and as soon as he put it into his pocket Tobias plunged his hand into his sporran and drew out a small purple bag.

'I have carried this for years without number,' he said, 'always in hope, but never in expectation. Finding the seventh son of a seventh son is an unlikely happenstance.'

'I don't know what you mean,' said Jake. 'I'm not a seventh son. I have four brothers. They're all older than me so I'm the fifth son.'

Tobias rested his hand reassuringly on Jake's shoulder. 'My boy,' he said, 'you will find that I am right. Not all babes are born to live and you are the seventh son your mother bore. More importantly, your father was a seventh son too, and his father before him, and so on, and so on, back into the mists of time, for it takes seven generations of seventh sons to awaken The Gift.'

Jake pointed at Merryn. 'But she's not a son. How did she get it?'

'Merryn's case is different. The Gift came through the female line from a wise woman who was also called Merryn MacQueen. It is a long story, and one which Merryn will share with you when the time is right.'

'I don't understand,' said Jake. 'I didn't ask for it and I don't think I want it. I don't even know what it means.'

'It means that you were born to join the fight against evil.'

Tobias opened the purple bag and took out an amethyst pendulum. It was larger than the pendants and identical to Merryn's.

'Wear it and it too will become invisible. It will protect you and allow you to contact me, should the need arise.'

Jake backed away. His mind was in a whirl. It might protect him, but that didn't mean it would protect Rex. 'I don't want it,' he said.

Tobias returned it to the purple bag. 'You need time to consider. This has come as a shock to you. If you are not ready to wear it, put it in your pocket. You have until this hour three days hence to decide.'

James looked at his watch. 'It's just twelve o'clock,' he said, 'so the deadline is noon on Tuesday.'

'Exactly so,' said Tobias. He turned back to Jake and continued with his explanation. 'If you do not wear it, it will return to me of its own accord. If that happens, those on the side of evil will be free to enlist your help. They may flatter you and tempt you. They may shower you with gifts and promise to make your dreams come true. On the other hand they may hurt you. They may threaten to harm something that you hold dear. But remember this. They cannot be trusted. In the end, when you have outlived your usefulness, they will destroy you.'

The other five sat still, stunned to silence, hanging onto every word that Tobias uttered. They watched as a mixture of emotions flickered across Jake's face. Surely, he'd wear the pendulum. The alternative was too awful to contemplate.

The suspense was too much for Hamish. 'Take it,' he urged. 'Take it and wear it. If I were you I'd jump at the chance. I wish I had The Gift. I'd be proud of it.'

'I know why you're hesitating,' said Merryn. 'Having The Gift is scary, but it'll help you to make the world a safer place, so it's got to be worth it. If you don't take the pendulum you'll still have The Gift, but without it you won't be protected.'

Jake put his arm round his dog's neck and buried his face in its fur. What could he do? Deep down inside he knew that Miss Turner was evil and that Tobias was speaking the truth, but he couldn't risk losing Rex. He would have to obey Miss Turner's instructions, but what could he say to Tobias?

Hamish opened his mouth to plead with Jake, but Tobias raised his hand to stop him. 'It is a serious matter for Jake,' he said. 'The decision must be his, and his alone.'

They sat in silence for several minutes until Jake eventually lifted his head.

'The thing is,' he said. 'I don't know what to believe. When I was a little kid I told my mum and dad about seeing ghosts, but they didn't believe me. They convinced me that it was all in my imagination. It didn't stop me seeing them, it just stopped me from talking about them.'

He looked up at Tobias, but found that he was unable to meet the wizard's eyes. 'I saw you appear out of nowhere, but I can't believe you're real. Perhaps you're like my ghosts, just in my imagination.'

He held out his hand for the pendulum. 'I don't think I can wear it,' he said, 'but I'll put it in my pocket and think about it.'

He turned away, and with Rex at his side he headed down the castle mound.

'You can't let him go,' said Merryn. 'Please, make him come back. Make him wear it.'

Tobias looked at her with eyes full of sadness. 'I cannot,' he said. 'Unlike the evil ones, I cannot use force. He is free to make his own decision.'

Jake left Kerrera with a heavy heart. He wanted to stay, to get to know Hamish and the others, to find out more about Tobias and The Benevolent Wizards. Most of all he wanted to wear the amethyst pendulum that lay in its purple bag at the bottom of his pocket. He'd always known that he was different from other people and now he knew why. If he had The Gift he wanted to use it. He called Rex to heel and slipped a lead onto his collar as they boarded the ferry back to the mainland.

He half expected the hateful Miss Turner to appear round a corner, or to pop up out of thin air, but there was no sign of her. He hurried back to Oban and made his way home, wondering what to say when he finally met her. Dare he tell her half a story? Would it be enough to say that the five children had hag-stones to protect them from witches? Would she sense that he too had a hag-stone, and that next to it, in his pocket, lay something even more powerful? Whatever else he told her, he decided not to tell her that he'd met a wizard.

He slept badly that night and when Sunday dawned he was reluctant to get out of bed. By mid-morning, Rex came up to his room, tugged at the duvet and pushed his wet nose into the curve of Jake's neck.

'OK,' Jake said. 'You win. We'll go out and if we meet the witchy woman. I'll tell her something. I'm not sure what, but let's get it over.'

Out they went, along the esplanade, keeping to areas that were busy with people. He didn't want to meet Miss Turner in a deserted corner where she could do something dreadful without anyone noticing. But Miss Turner did not appear.

Chapter 17

When Monday morning arrived Jake transferred the hag-stone and the amethyst pendulum to the pocket of his school trousers. He left Rex in the house and went to school expecting to see Miss Turner. To his relief, Miss Turner was not there.

'Unfortunately,' said Mr Cummins, 'our student has not recovered from her accident so she will not be returning.'

'Yes!' Hamish wanted to shout at the top of his voice. He wanted to punch the air, jump on his desk and do a triumphant dance, but he managed to sit still and mask his delight with a cough.

He looked across the room. Jake's shoulders had dropped as if he'd let out a huge sigh of relief. It hadn't been obvious before, but Hamish was certain now. Miss Turner had some sort of hold over Jake. She must have threatened him with something horrible. That's why he was reluctant to wear the amethyst pendulum. But Tobias must have got rid of her, so now everything would be fine.

Hamish's triumph was short-lived, because Mr Cummins hadn't finished speaking. 'Miss Twitchley, another student will join us during the morning.'

'Twitchley!' Hamish gasped. Miss Turner hadn't been eliminated at all. He should have guessed. Three names beginning with T—Turner, Twitchley, Twitch. The woman's identity was obvious now. She was Mandragora Twitch in yet another disguise.

At break time he told Rosie to take a hag-stone out of the bag that Tobias had given him. She hesitated before putting in her hand and pulling out a small stone with a hole through it.

'What's it for and what am I supposed to do with it?' she asked as she turned it over in her palm.

'Just keep it with you,' said Hamish. 'If you'd had it before, Clickfinger couldn't have harmed you. It's a protection against witches.'

'But there aren't any...' She stopped and looked at him with wide anxious eyes. 'Are you saying my story was true and that there's another witch about?'

Hamish nodded. 'Put it in your pocket and I'll explain later. I've got to find Peter and Jake before the next lesson.'

He turned away quickly and although he broke the rules and ran along the corridor he was too late. Mr Cummins had already arrived for their English lesson. Peter and Jake were in their places and there was no time to speak to either of them. He hoped that Miss Twitchley would stay away until he'd warned them. But it was not to be. Just before the end of the lesson, an extremely tall, fierce-looking woman strode into the classroom.

'Twitchley,' she said as she grasped Mr Cummins by the hand, 'your new student.'

Mr Cummins stared up at the woman who was a head taller than himself. His hand was shaken vigorously and when Miss Twitchley finally let go he stepped back in shock.

Miss Twitchley searched the faces in front of her. When she came to Hamish she raised one eyebrow. 'There's a familiar face,' she said. 'Young MacQueen, I believe, and Jake too. How very nice to meet old friends.'

Jake's chair screeched as he pushed it back. He leaned on the desk to steady himself. 'I'm ... I'm going to be sick,' he gasped as he dashed for the door.

Hamish leapt to his feet, chased after him and called over his shoulder. 'I'll make sure he's all right.'

When Hamish reached the boys' toilets, Jake was leaning over the washbasin, retching violently. Hamish put one hand on his shoulder, but Jake shrugged him away. He coughed, spluttered and threw up his breakfast. Then he staggered backwards and sat down on the floor with his head between his knees.

'Listen,' said Hamish as he sat down beside him. 'I know what's going on. Miss Twitchley is a witch. Her real name is Mandragora Twitch and last time we saw her she was Miss Turner.'

Jake's shoulders started to shake. He sniffed and snuffled and struggled to hold back his tears. Strangled sounds came out of his mouth, but he couldn't form them into words.

'I know why you followed us to Kerrera.' Hamish continued. 'I bet she's blackmailing you. She's going to do something nasty to you if you don't spy on us.'

Jake shook his head violently and burst into tears. 'Not to me,' he sobbed, 'to my dog.' His voice rose to a wail. 'She's going to kill him if I don't tell her what you do.'

'No, she jolly well isn't,' said Hamish. 'Listen. It's nearly lunchtime. Can we get to your house and back before afternoon school?'

Jake nodded.

'Stay here,' said Hamish, 'and don't come out for anything. I need my school bag. I'll be back in a minute.'

The bell rang to mark the end of the morning. Hamish peered round the corner and waited until Mr Cummins and Miss Twitchley had left the classroom. He dashed inside, grabbed his bag and ran back to the toilets. Jake was still sitting on the floor, but when he saw Hamish, he wiped his eyes on his sleeve and struggled to his feet. They hurried out of school and dashed up the hill. Ten minutes later they went into Jake's house where Rex, with his tail wagging furiously, rushed to greet them.

'Quick,' said Hamish, 'get some strong string.'

'What for?' Jake asked.

'Just get it,' said Hamish. 'We haven't got all day and you'll see in a minute.'

By the time Jake returned with a ball of string, Hamish had tipped the remaining hag-stones from his bag. Although they'd been intended for the other children, this was an emergency. He slipped the string through the hole in the first hag-stone and tied a double knot. Then he did the same with the others. Lastly he wound the string round Rex's collar and tied both ends tightly to the buckle.

When that was done he put his hand on his crystal pendant and called Tobias. 'Emergency,' he said. 'It's Twitch. She was Miss Turner and now she's back as Miss Twitchley.'

'Mandragora Twitch!' Tobias exclaimed. 'Of all the witches, she is the most accomplished at changing her appearance. I am afraid that eliminating her is not going to be easy. We will have to try again. I am sorry. We thought we had succeeded. Do you know why she returned?'

'She told Jake to steal something that belongs to Emily. I think she wants to put her under a spell, and she's making him spy on us. She wants to know everything we do and everything we say. If he doesn't she's going to kill his dog. I've made a collar with the rest of the hag-stones and I've put it round the dog's neck. We have to go back to school now and Twitch is there, but I don't know what to do next.'

'You have done well, Hamish,' said Tobias. 'Tell Jake that Rex is safe. Twitch will not be able to harm him, but do not leave Emily alone. I think The Grand High Witch has plans for her. That is all you can do. The rest is up to Jake.'

Jake, with his arms round Rex's neck, had been listening anxiously to the one-sided conversation. He had heard Hamish's words but had no idea about the response.

'That was Tobias,' said Hamish. 'Rex will be safe, but Twitchley will be furious when she realises she can't harm him. She won't give in though. She'll think of another way to blackmail you.'

Jake started to panic. 'But how can I stop her? Tell me what to do.'

'I can't,' said Hamish. 'You have to decide for yourself.'

Once again Jake buried his face in Rex's fur. Then he stood up and took the purple bag from his pocket. He tipped the amethyst pendulum into his hand and held it up by its silver chain. He watched the rays of purple light sweeping the corners of the room and he slipped the chain over his head. He crossed to the mirror and looked at his reflection. It was true. The pendulum was now invisible. He fingered it to make sure it was still there, and as he did so, he heard the voice of Tobias.

'Well done, my boy. You have made a brave choice.'

Hamish heard the voice too. He slapped Jake on the back and gave a whoop of joy. 'Welcome,' he said. 'Now you're one of us.'

'Do not get too excited,' said Tobias. 'A dangerous task awaits you at the end of the school day. I want Hamish, Merryn, James, Peter and Emily to go to McCaig's Tower. Jake, you must go home, wait a while, then take Rex and his ball to the tower.'

'Then what?' asked Hamish.

'Miss Twitchley will follow Jake. The five of you must be at the tower before her. Merryn will know what to do. Tell her that I will join you as soon as I can.'

Chapter 18

Everything was going to plan, but as she walked up to McCaig's Tower, Merryn couldn't chase the worried frown from her face. She knew that Jake was wearing the amethyst pendulum, that Rex had a hag-stone necklace and that Miss Twitchley was likely to follow them. Tobias expected her to know what to do, but she hadn't a clue. How could she instruct the others when her mind was blank? But all the worrying was pointless because everything came clear when she stepped under the archway.

'Hide in the bushes,' she said, 'and when I step out you must follow. When I take out my crystal you must do the same. Now, go quickly before Jake arrives.'

Within seconds they'd all disappeared, and a few minutes later Jake stepped onto the grass with Rex. He walked up and down, looking anxiously this way and that, but the others were so well hidden that he couldn't see them. He ran to the archway to see if they were coming, but there was no sign of them on the path.

Merryn could see that he was beginning to panic. He looked as if he was going to run away and she had to stop him.

'Pssst,' she whispered. 'We're here. Try to act normally. Play with Rex.'

Jake did as he was told, but he was afraid to send the ball too far in case he lost sight of Rex. The hag-stones were supposed to protect him, but he couldn't quite believe that a few stones would stop Miss

Twitchley's terrible spells. Now he would find out, for her voice called out from somewhere behind him. His body stiffened and he grabbed Rex by the collar.

'How very nice to meet you, Jake. I have discarded Miss Turner, but I expect you realise that she and I are one and the same.' She gave a low chuckle. 'I want to hear the password though, just to make sure you remember it.'

Jake's free hand flew to the amethyst pendulum. He could feel it vibrating, warning him that the woman was indeed a witch. When he turned round, he didn't need warning. Now that he was wearing the pendulum he didn't need to peer through half-closed eyes. He could see through Miss Twitchley's disguise to the ghastly hag that lay beneath. He stepped back in horror. He opened his mouth to speak, but all that came out was a croak.

'The password,' she said through clenched teeth, 'and I will not wait.'

Jake swallowed hard and coughed to clear his throat. 'Goodbye,' he wheezed.

'That's only half of it,' snapped Miss Twitchley. 'I've been looking forward to hearing it. Don't disappoint me.'

Jake coughed again and shook his head. He caught a glimpse of Merryn in the bushes behind Miss Twitchley and he felt a sudden surge of confidence.

'Never,' he said. 'I'll never say it. I know who you are and you know who I am so there's no need for a password.'

Miss Twitchley frowned. 'That depends,' she said. 'If you've brought something from the girl Emily I might forget about the password.'

'I haven't brought anything,' said Jake. 'I don't steal.'

'In that case,' she said. 'I'll say the password for you. Goodbye, Rex.'

Her long warty nose twitched in Rex's direction, but Rex didn't fall over. He stood facing her with his tail wagging and his mouth open as if he was laughing. She twitched her nose again and moved towards him. Twitch, twitch, went her nose. Wag, wag went Rex's tail. She put out her hand to grab him, but the hag-stones forced her back.

'You think you can get the better of me with a few hag-stones,' she shrieked. 'Well, you can think again. Tell me what you found out about those pesky brats, or I'll do something worse than put a spell on your dog.'

'No,' said Jake. 'They're not pesky brats. They're my friends and I will not spy on them.'

'Friends,' she sneered. 'Fine friends they are. Where are they when you need them?'

'Here,' said Merryn as she stepped out of the bushes with Hamish, James, Peter and Emily.

'Quick, make a circle round her,' she said, 'but not too close.'

Trapped by the hag-stones, Miss Twitchley didn't know which way to turn. She dashed from one side of the circle to the other. She tried to break through the gaps between the children, but they stood their ground. They no longer saw the frantic figure of Miss Twitchley as she stumbled about in her high-heeled shoes. To them all, through the power of the amethysts, they saw an ugly black-clad witch with her grey hair flying.

'Now,' said Merryn as she took hold of the silver chain and pulled out her amethyst pendulum.

The others did the same, and although the crystals were invisible, their purple rays focused on the witch in the centre of their circle. Cursing furiously, she fell to her knees and tried to hide her eyes from the glare.

Merryn was wondering what to do next, when, to her great relief, Tobias appeared and took his place between her and Jake.

'Mandragora Twitch,' he said. 'Remember this. You did not gain The Book of Spells. You did not win The Clickfinger Locket. Your plan to capture Emily has failed. These brave children have overpowered you. Get to your feet and return to The Grand High Witch. Tell her that Benevolent Wizardry will not tolerate the use of children to further her evil ends.'

He gave a grim smile. 'Also tell her that we have the greatest of allies. We hold The Clickfinger Locket and it has not forgotten the humiliation suffered by Ammonia Begonia Clickfinger. Nor has it forgotten that The Snake Wand was responsible for her elimination. I have reason to believe that it is eager for revenge.'

'Step back,' he said to the six children. 'Cover your crystals and let this despicable creature go.'

'But,' Hamish stuttered. 'What... what if she comes back?'

'It is a risk,' said Tobias, 'but an extremely slight one. She will not forget what happened this day.'

The children slipped their crystals inside their clothing and the rays of purple light vanished. Mandragora staggered and with a wail of anguish she disappeared. Up on the wall of the tower, two ravens croaked as they took to the air. Tobias watched as they flew away.

'Witch Watchers,' he said. 'They know all that has occurred. They will report back to The Grand High Witch. If Mandragora tries to lie, or fails to convey my message, she will be exposed as a cheat and a liar.'

As he finished speaking, Rosie, looking very anxious and more than a little afraid, scrambled out of the bushes. She looked from one to the other and then she went to Tobias.

'I remember you,' she said in a hesitant whisper. 'You don't look quite the same but I know your voice. You were in Gylen Castle and I know I can trust you because you helped us to escape.'

Tobias put his hand on her shoulder. 'It is good to see you again, Rosie, but tell me what brought you here.'

She looked round at the other children. 'I'm sorry,' she said, 'I didn't mean to butt in, but I knew you were up to something. After you left, Miss Twitchley tried to grab me. She would have too, if Hamish hadn't given me a hag-stone. I'd heard him telling Peter to go to McCaig's Tower after school, so as soon as Miss Twitchley left me, I came to see what was happening. It was so scary that I wish I hadn't, but I was in the castle like the rest of you. Well, not quite all of you.' She pointed at Jake. 'He wasn't there, but he's mixed up in it somehow. I suppose I'd better go now. I'm sorry. I shouldn't have come.'

It was a long speech. She came to an embarrassed halt and turned away. Merryn and Emily each grabbed a hand to stop her from leaving.

'We can't let her go,' said Hamish.

'No, we can't,' said James. 'She's definitely one of us.'

'And if Twitchley tried to catch her,' said Peter, 'she needs protecting.'

'She does indeed,' said Tobias.' He opened his sporran, took out another amethyst pendant and slipped it over Rosie's head.

'This is for you,' he said. 'It has the same qualities as the ones worn by the others. I have much to tell you all, so Hamish can explain its purpose later. Come, make a circle and join hands.'

He took Merryn's hand in his left hand and Jake's hand in his right and the other five took their places in between.

Your strength grows as your numbers increase,' he said. 'Now there are seven of you, and as Jake knows, seven is an extremely powerful number.'

Chapter 19

'Sit with me,' said Tobias, 'for I have much to tell, and more to ask. Failure to destroy The Great Wizard has left Malevolent Witchery in turmoil. The Grand High Witch will be furious when Mandragora Twitch returns without Emily. I foresee arguments and disagreements. Their attention will no longer be focused on us, so the time is right to do battle.'

'Do you think you can win?' asked Merryn.

Tobias lifted both hands in a gesture of uncertainty. 'I must believe that we can, otherwise there is no point in trying. But we cannot win on our own. The Gift means that Merryn and Jake are honour-bound to help us. And because it combines the wisdom of the first Merryn MacQueen and the power of the Selkie Folk, the necklace of sea-beans and hag-stones is essential to our success. I now need to know if I can count on the rest of you.'

'I'll do what I can,' said Hamish as he looked at the others, 'I've been helping ever since Merryn got The Gift. I'm not going to stop now.'

'Being trapped in Clickfinger's fortress was awful,' said Emily. 'It scared me stiff, but we won. We got the better of her and I'm proud of what I did. If I can help to get rid of more people like her, I'll help too.'

'You have every right to be proud,' said Tobias. 'If you had not released me from that dreadful collar we would not be here today.'

James and Peter looked at one another uncertainly. Rosie, who'd missed the Saturday trip to Kerrera frowned and clenched her fists. She hadn't heard the whole story and she wanted to know more before she made up her mind.

'For James, Peter and Rosie,' said Tobias, 'the situation is difficult. They experienced the horror of transformation so I am not surprised that they are wary.' He turned to the three of them. 'But now that you have hag-stones and crystals you are protected.'

'But not from a whole gang of witches, and not from The Grand High Witch,' said James. 'We saw them all on Witchvision and we know what The Snake Wand can do.'

'You are right,' Tobias said with a sigh, 'but against single witches I truly believe that you are safe. To meet more than one at the same time would be unusual in the extreme. Remember, Mandragora could not break through the hag-stones that Rex was wearing. Your crystals are far more powerful than hag-stones and you saw how she cowered before them.

'It's a risk,' said Peter, 'but we can't let the witches win.'

'I daren't promise in case I can't do it,' said Rosie, 'but I'll try my best.'

'I will too,' said James, 'but I couldn't bear to be a slug again.'

'Nor could I,' added Peter, 'but I'll help.'

Jake stared at James with a look of horror on his face. 'A slug!' he exclaimed. 'What on earth are you talking about?'

'Clickfinger captured children,' said Merryn, 'not just these three, but dozens of others. If they annoyed her she changed them into creatures and put them in cages. Emily didn't annoy her so she stayed as a girl.

She rescued some of the others and then Hamish and I went to help.'

'And The Grand High Witch eliminated Clickfinger,' said Hamish, 'and all her spells came undone so we escaped.'

'Not at all bad for a summary,' said Tobias, 'but when you have time, Merryn, you must tell the full story. Now, let us forget the past and look to the future. Besides protecting yourselves and reporting sightings of witches I need you to discover The Grand High Witch's greatest secret.'

'Just like that,' said James. 'Easy peasy, let's go and ask her.'

'Don't joke,' said Emily. 'It's serious.'

Tobias turned to Emily. 'Indeed it is,' he said, 'and you should know the nature of it.'

Emily tried to think, but nothing came into her head. 'You'll have to give me a clue,' she said.

'It has something to do with names,' said Tobias.

'Names,' Emily exclaimed, 'of course. When I asked Ammonia what the B stood for she was furious. She said that knowing a person's full name gives you power over them. She had power over me because she knew my full name was Emily Elizabeth Carmichael.'

Merryn agreed. 'That's why The Grand High Witch shouted Ammonia Begonia Clickfinger just before she eliminated her.'

'And why The Clickfinger Locket said Vitriola Pustula Sniff when it did the same to her,' said Hamish.

'So we just have to find The Grand High Witch's true name,' said Jake, 'then we can get rid of her too. That shouldn't be too difficult, should it? I mean...' He stopped abruptly when he saw the expressions of disbelief on all their faces.

'If you'd seen her you wouldn't say that,' said Merryn. 'Of course it'll be difficult—and dangerous too.'

They all began talking at once, but no one listened to anyone else. Tobias let them chatter for a while before calling for silence.

'Merryn is right. It is the most difficult challenge of all,' he said, 'for there are few, if any, who remember who she was before she became The Grand High Witch. Somewhere in The Annals of Malevolent Witchery her first and last names will be written down, but middle names are only ever recorded by their initial letter.'

'I bet they're protected by a powerful spell,' said James. 'Is there any chance of breaking it?'

'Not a hope,' said Hamish, 'and even if we could it wouldn't help with her middle name.'

'No,' Tobias agreed, but if we discover the initial letter we may be able to work it out. There are often patterns in names, rhymes like Ammonia Begonia, or words ending with similar letters like Vitriola Pustula. All seven of you must travel far and wide to ask the help of Fairy Folk and Selkies.'

Seven mouths opened in shock. Seven pairs of eyes stared at Tobias as if they couldn't believe what they were hearing.

'You've forgotten that we have to go to school,' said James.

'And even if we hadn't,' said Peter 'we can't wander all over the place without our parents knowing.'

'I have not forgotten anything,' said Tobias. 'Now you are seven you can travel through space and time in the blink of an eye. You can take yourselves to any place you wish, and when you return, time will not have moved by a single second.'

Exclamations of surprise and excitement filled the air and once again Tobias called for silence.

'I will show you what to do,' he said. 'It is a simple procedure, but remember this. It will only work if all seven of you are of the same mind. I shouldn't need to remind you to wear your crystals and carry your hag-stones at all times for they are vital to your safety. But in addition to that, the Travel Magic will not work if any one of them is missing. Merryn's necklace of sea-beans and hag-stones is essential too. Now, I want you to make a circle by crossing your arms and joining hands.'

'Like when we sing 'Auld Lang Syne' at Hogmanay?' Rosie asked.

'That is correct for the return journey,' said Tobias, 'but for the first part of the journey you will face outwards. When you are ready, Merryn will say the name of the place you wish to visit. You will be transported to that place immediately. When your task is completed, you must face inwards, cross your arms and join hands again. When Merryn says 'back', you will return to the place from which you started. Now you must practise. Go to Ganavan Sands and return without delay.'

'What about Rex?' asked Jake.

'He won't miss you,' said Tobias. 'He will be here when you return, but it is a good point. Make sure that he isn't in the middle of the circle when you leave. If he is, he will travel with you and if he strays you may not be able to bring him back. Now go.'

The seven children crossed their arms and joined hands in an outward facing circle.

'Ganavan Sands,' said Merryn.

Miraculously, they were there, standing by the sea, looking at one another with expressions of amazement and delight. It was tempting to stay, to chase across the beach and admire the views of Mull and Lismore, but there were instructions to obey. So they crossed their arms and joined hands in an inward facing circle.

'Back,' said Merryn, and they stood in the middle of McCaig's Tower as if they'd never been away.

'Excellent,' said Tobias. 'Now I must leave you in Merryn's capable hands. She will be your leader because she knows the nature of the task. She also knows who to ask for help. Contact me if the need arises, but remember that I too will be busy making plans and seeking answers. Take care of one another until we meet again.'

Before anyone could reply, Tobias Witchbane had disappeared and they were left wondering if it had all been a dream.

'Crumbs,' said Hamish as he looked at his sister. 'I hope you really do know what to do because I haven't a clue.'

Chapter 20

Mandragora Twitch was terrified of returning to The Grand High Witch. She fled to her hideout, a cosy den that she'd created inside Carraig Fhada lighthouse at the end of Port Ellen Bay on the Isle of Islay. She looked out on the sea, on the coast of Ireland to the south and on Kintyre to the east. If no one knew her whereabouts, she could stay hidden forever, but if The Grand High Witch discovered where she was, she knew she'd be arrested and eliminated.

'I've been a fool,' she muttered. 'The other witches were right to refuse The Grand High Witch's challenge. I shouldn't have said that capturing Emily would be easy. I should have done it in secret and produced her as a surprise.'

She sighed and twiddled the long strands of greasy hair around her first finger. 'I can't hide for the rest of my life so I suppose I'll have to go back. If she lets me explain I might just get away with it.'

A shudder ran down her back as she remembered the children, their amethyst lights blinding her, forcing her to her knees, blocking her ability to fight back. She couldn't understand why Tobias Witchbane had made them release her. His message for The Grand High Witch didn't seem a good enough reason for sparing her life. Still, she was grateful, even though the thought of delivering the message turned her legs to jelly. If she'd been a dog she would have crawled on her belly with her tail between her legs. But she wasn't a dog and the thought of acting like one made her pull herself together.

'I won't grovel,' she said as she leapt to her feet. 'I won't bow my head in shame. The other witches can taunt me, but I don't care. I'll tell The Grand High Witch that not even she could capture Emily. I'll get the others on my side and then I'll stand a chance.'

She knew that in three days time, the witches would get together for their monthly gathering in McCaig's Tower. She spent the intervening days wandering along Singing Sands, talking to herself, rehearsing what she was going to say. In the evenings she looked out from the lighthouse, staring absent-mindedly at the flashes from the Rathlin lighthouses across the stretch of sea.

When the time came to leave she knew what she had to say and she was feeling confident. But when she saw The Snake Wand, the blood drained from her face and the carefully rehearsed words disappeared from her brain. And when The Grand High Witch frowned, her knees began to tremble.

'You promised to bring the girl, Emily,' said The Grand High Witch. 'How dare you return without her?'

'I tried my best,' said Mandragora. 'No-one could have done more. I was close, but...'

'Not close enough,' snapped The Grand High Witch. 'You failed. You thought by pleasing me that you could worm your way into The Grand High Council.' She laughed. 'You have not pleased me so you can forget it. We have no room for failures.'

Mandragora staggered as if she'd been punched in the stomach. 'But that's not fair,' she gasped.

'Who do you think you are?' roared The Grand High Witch. 'It is not your place to tell me what is fair.'

Mandragora tried to answer, but The Snake Wand flicked its forked tongue and although she mouthed the words, no sound came with them.

'You have one more day to bring the girl,' yelled The Grand High Witch, 'or stay away for good. Now we retire for lunch and you would be wise to leave before we return.'

The Grand High Council left the stage and the other witches took out their packed lunches. To Mandragora's surprise, not one of them taunted her for failing. She heard a lot of muttering about The Grand High Witch being unfair. She heard someone say that members of The Council were tired of her bossiness.

'My grandmother is on The Council,' said one young witch. 'She says The Grand High Witch would be powerless without The Snake Wand.'

'That's what I heard,' said another. 'If anyone disagrees with her she just waves The Snake Wand and gets everything she wants. There's no point in having a Grand High Council because she ignores them.'

'She's been in power too long,' said an elderly witch. 'She was Grand High Witch when I was a girl.'

'Then it's time to get rid of her,' said Mandragora, 'but we'll have to destroy The Snake Wand first.'

There was uproar as opinions and suggestions flew from one witch to another. Heads shook and voices declared that the task was impossible.

'The Snake Wand is invincible,' said the oldest witch.

'If that's true,' said Mandragora, 'we must find another way. Does anyone know The Grand High Witch's real name?'

Silence fell. It was a dangerous subject. The witches questioned one another in whispers, but no one had any idea of The Grand High Witch's true identity. Mandragora raised her arm and caught the attention of every witch in the room.

'We need a revolution,' she declared, 'an uprising, an election to replace The Grand High Witch.'

'Hear! Hear!'

'Bravo!'

Cries of approval came from every corner of the vast room. Mandragora flung both arms in the air. The voices died away and every single witch waited to hear what she had to say.

'I failed to capture Emily,' she said, 'because The Benevolent Wizards are protecting her. I cannot capture or harm her. I cannot even touch her.'

'Hag-stones,' called a voice from the crowd.

'Far more than hag-stones,' said Mandragora. 'Tobias Witchbane, brother of The Great Wizard is behind it, and Emily is not alone. There are other children and they all have something of great power. That is bad enough, but there is something else.' She paused to make sure that everyone was listening. 'The Benevolent Wizards have taken possession of The Clickfinger Locket.'

There was an audible gasp as all the witches drew in their breath.

'I was close to getting it,' Mandragora continued, 'and so was Vitriola Sniff, but when she tried to grab it, it destroyed her.'

There was another gasp.

'It would have destroyed me too, but I decided on another plan. I studied The Benevolent Wizards and discovered that their strength lies not in numbers as we previously thought.'

'Then where does it lie?' asked the oldest witch.

'In co-operation,' said Mandragora. 'They work together and that is why they succeed. I have watched them, I have followed them and I have dedicated myself to their downfall. We will follow their example. I will be The Grand High Witch and if you all work with me I will lead Malevolent Witchery to victory.

The witches rose to their feet. They cheered and stamped their approval.

'Mandragora Twitch for Grand High Witch,' they chanted.

'Stand by me,' Mandragora cried, 'and we will overthrow The Grand High Witch. We will defeat The Benevolent Wizards. We will rule the world.'

The chanting grew to a crescendo. 'Mandragora Twitch for Grand High Witch,' cried the witches.

Behind Mandragora, The Grand High Witch and members of The Council returned to the stage. The voices from the hall faltered. The witches returned to their seats in terrified silence. Mandragora turned as The Grand High Witch came towards her. The Snake Wand writhed and hissed. Its red eyes flashed and its forked tongue flickered.

'You have gone too far,' snarled The Grand High Witch.

She pointed The Snake Wand at the audience. 'You have all gone too far.'

The witches cowered in their seats, their faces turned pale for they knew their lives were in danger. Mandragora refused to back down. She knew what she had to do. She knew it was an enormous risk, but she had to take it.

'I promised to lead you to victory,' she said to the audience. 'I ask you again. Stand by me and we will rule the world.'

The oldest witch rose to her feet. 'I will stand by you,' she said. 'We need a new leader with new methods. We need Mandra...'

The Grand High Witch pointed The Snake Wand at the speaker. The red eyes flashed, the forked tongue sent out its deadly venom and the oldest witch staggered, fell and vanished in a puff of dust.

'Does anyone else dare to challenge me?' The Grand High Witch asked.

Not a single voice broke the silence. Mandragora shook her head in despair. She knew she'd be eliminated, but she would speak her mind first.

'You've outlived your usefulness,' she sneered. 'You rule by The Snake Wand. Without it you are nothing. Go on, destroy me, but mark my words, you will regret my passing.'

She drew herself up to her full height and faced The Snake Wand. 'Mandragora Malodora Twitch,' cried The Grand High Witch. 'Prepare to meet your doom.'

The Snake Wand hissed. Mandragora whirled into the air with her cloak flapping around her. She grew smaller and smaller and smaller. But until she disappeared completely, her voice continued to call curses on the head of The Grand High Witch.

Chapter 21

Unaware that Mandragora Twitch had been eliminated, Merryn told the others to keep looking for her.

'Of course she'll be in a different disguise,' she said, 'but your crystals will vibrate and if that happens you must get out of her way and call Tobias. But that's not all. We need the name of The Grand High Witch and we must ask The Fairy Woman for help.'

'Great,' Hamish exclaimed. 'She's on Tiree, so we'll have to use Travel Magic.'

Merryn looked round at the others. Rosie stared at her with big round eyes. Jake crouched down and put his arm round Rex's neck. James and Peter, with frowns on their faces, edged closer together. Emily shrugged as if she didn't know what to think.

Only Hamish had a look of sheer delight on his face. 'Come on,' he said, 'what are we waiting for?'

'We can't go now,' said Peter. 'We have homework and it's nearly tea-time.'

'So what?' said Hamish. 'It'll be exactly the same time when we get back.'

Merryn listened to each of their comments in turn. She understood the fear of the unknown. Using Travel Magic to go down the road to Ganavan Sands was one thing, using it to cross miles of sea was another matter.

'I'd go on my own if I could,' she said.

'Not without me,' said Jake.

'Nor me,' said Hamish, 'and you can't go by yourself, anyway. You heard what Tobias said.'

'He's right,' said Emily. 'It has to be all seven of us.'

'I'm not keen' said James, 'but if we've got to go, it might as well be now.'

'So,' said Rosie as she grabbed Peter's hand, 'let's do it.'

Seconds later they stood in their outward-facing circle, arms crossed, hands held tightly together.

'Fang an t-Sithean, Tiree,' said Merryn.

There was no sense of speed, no notion of rushing air, no impression of travelling over the ocean. Without time to blink an eye or take a breath they found themselves on Tiree. The low mound of Fang an t-Sithean rose before them. Merryn signalled to the others to stay outside the circle of stones while she walked through a gap between them. She climbed up to the rocky outcrop, but before she reached the top, The Fairy Woman appeared and called a greeting.

'Welcome, Merryn MacQueen, I foresaw your coming and I must congratulate you on your victory over the witch of Tiree.'

Merryn bowed her head respectfully. 'That seems a long time ago,' she said, 'and without your heart-stone we would have failed.'

'Not so,' said The Fairy Woman, 'without your faith and bravery the heart-stone would have been powerless. It was a combined effort, and you prevented the witch of Tiree from waging war on me and my people.'

She glanced down the mound and counted the waiting children. 'I see that there are seven of you,' she said, 'and I believe your magical powers are even greater than before.'

She beckoned to the others and waited until they stood before her. 'If you are friends of Merryn,' she said, 'you are friends of mine. I remember you, Hamish, but know nothing of the others.' Her glance settled on Jake. 'Yet there is something familiar about this one.'

'He has The Gift,' said Merryn.

'Ah!' The Fairy Woman smiled. 'It is good to know that you are no longer alone, but what of the other four?'

As briefly as she could, Merryn explained about Clickfinger and all that had happened in the magical fortress inside Gylen Castle.

The Fairy Woman nodded wisely. 'Defeating that particular witch was no mean feat,' she said. 'Now I understand what binds you all together, but that is not why you are here.'

'No,' said Merryn, and she told of Clickfinger's attempt to kill The Great Wizard at The Festival of Malevolent Witchery. 'Now we have to defeat The Malevolent Witches once and for all, but for that, we need your help.'

'I will help if it lies within my power,' said The Fairy Woman, 'but first, tell me what form of magic brought you here.'

'Travel Magic.' Hamish clicked his fingers. 'It's as quick as winking. Tobias taught us how to do it.'

The Fairy Woman smiled at his enthusiasm. 'Then The Benevolent Wizards sent you to make a request on their behalf.'

She turned back to Merryn. 'Tell me what you need.'

'It sounds simple, but I know it isn't,' said Merryn. 'We have to find the true name of The Grand High Witch.'

Exclamations of surprise and ripples of laughter came from deep beneath their feet. Jake, Emily, James, Peter and Rosie stepped back and stared at the ground in shock.

'Do not be afraid,' said The Fairy Woman. 'My people doubt the success of your mission. They know that the middle names of witches are closely guarded secrets. They know too, that The Grand High Witch has outlived almost everyone in the world of magic, but I will call my Elders and see if they can help.'

No sooner had she finished speaking than three old women appeared at her side. Like The Fairy Woman, they wore long green skirts covered by crisp white aprons. Next came three bearded men in knee britches and waistcoats of the same green. Their shirts and stockings were white and the silver buckles on their black shoes shone in the late afternoon sunlight. One of them stooped and leant on a curiously carved walking stick. His bright blue eyes flickered over the children and he raised his eyebrows questioningly.

The Fairy Woman rested her hand on his shoulder. 'You are the oldest of us all,' she said. 'Can you tell these brave children the true name of The Grand High Witch?'

Merryn and the others watched expectantly. Slowly, The Fairy Man shook his head. 'Alas. I cannot. It all happened long ago, even before the time of my birth.' He scratched his head with his one free hand. 'But...'

'But what?' Hamish couldn't hold back the question.

The Fairy Man looked at him and smiled. 'I see you are eager for an answer, but I do not know it, and yet...'

The seven children watched as puzzled expressions flitted across the old man's face.

'And yet,' he said at last. 'There is something in the deep recesses of my mind. Some memory, something I overheard when I was a boy. The Elders were discussing the power of The Grand High Witch and yes... it comes to me now. One of them called her an upstart. He said that one of her Clan should never have risen to such a high state. Another one said that she won The Snake Wand by foul means and that without it she was practically powerless.'

He paused and shook his head. 'I am sorry. I cannot tell you more.'

The children sighed with disappointment, but despite the feeling of hopelessness that washed over her, Merryn managed to remember her manners.

'Thank you for trying,' she said.

'Take heart,' said The Fairy Woman. 'You may not have learned her name but you now know that she comes from one of the weaker Clans.'

'But we don't know what that means,' said Merryn.

'Making magic by means of a wand is the most powerful method of all,' said The Fairy Woman. 'Wands used correctly are formidable weapons. They transmit spells as quick as lightning and their aim is accurate.'

'So she won't be a 'Wand',' said Merryn.

'Nor a 'Clickfinger',' said The Fairy Woman. 'They are almost as deadly, and she will not be a 'Word' because they are the third most powerful Clan. They can project their spells with great accuracy and the use of the voice leaves the hands free for other mischief. No, I think we must look to lesser Clans.'

'Such as 'Sniffs'?' asked Hamish. 'And 'Twitches'. When Vitriola and Mandragora had a fight they sniffed and twitched like anything. It was easy to see which Clans they belonged to.'

'Indeed yes,' said The Fairy Woman, 'but those who use facial expressions can only work their spells when they are facing in the right direction. They are at a disadvantage when their backs are turned.'

'Let me get this straight,' said Jake. 'Are you saying that if we watch The Grand High Witch we'll be able to see how she makes her magic?'

Before anyone else could reply, Hamish provided the answer. 'No,' he said. 'She makes her magic with The Snake Wand, but if...' He grinned as he realised the significance of what he was about to say. 'If something happens to The Snake Wand she won't be able to use it. She'll have to use her own magic and we'll be able to see how she does it. So the most important thing isn't finding her name, it's destroying The Snake Wand. The trouble is, we can only do that if we discover the secret of its power.'

'Or its weakness,' said Merryn.

'Exactly,' said The Fairy Woman. 'Discover that, destroy it and Malevolent Witchery will start to crumble.'

'Impossible.' The oldest fairy man shook his head. 'Even if we knew the secret of The Snake Wand we could not get close enough to destroy it. We risk our lives by even looking at it, and who among us is brave enough to do that?'

Chapter 22

Merryn wished she was brave enough to face The Snake Wand, but she'd seen the red glow of its eyes. She'd watched the flicker of its forked tongue. She'd seen the clothes that were left behind when Ammonia Begonia Clickfinger was eliminated. It had all been on Witchvision, and that had been terrifying enough. The thought of actually meeting it face to face set her heart tattooing. Her breath came in shaky little puffs, and to make things worse, they were all looking at her as if it was her job to make the decisions. Every face was wide-eyed with fear and uncertainty.

Her voice came out in a croak. She coughed, swallowed and tried again. 'A single person would be eliminated in no time,' she said. 'We must stay together. Surely, if we do that, she can't destroy us all.'

'Brave words,' said The Fairy Woman, 'but you are wrong. In any case, the time may not be of your choosing. If it is, we can fight at your side. But if a meeting comes by chance you must be prepared to act alone.'

'Not alone,' said Jake. 'Wherever Travel Magic takes us, there'll always be seven of us.'

'Then we will do all we can to prepare and protect you,' said The Fairy Woman. 'Ours is a small community, but all over Scotland there are others. Someone, somewhere, must have the answer. I will send out messengers. Hopefully, one of them will return with something to our advantage, but you too must join the search.'

She turned to Merryn and continued. 'You are already acquainted with Roane, The Selkie. You must ask him to search beneath the sea. There are others too, who wish to put an end to Malevolent Witchery. Seek them out and ask each one for a Token, something powerful to add to your necklace, your crystals and your hag-stones. These things will help you in the final fight if those who lend them are unable to be with you.'

The Fairy Woman put her hand into the pocket of her apron. 'Take this,' she said. 'It is our contribution.'

Merryn watched her pull out a bag of purple silk. 'The heart-stone,' she gasped. 'Are you really going to lend it to us? You may need it and it could be ages before we can send it back to you.'

'That is as it may be,' said The Fairy Woman. 'Your need is greater than ours. You know the rules. Leave it in the bag until your time of greatest need, and when you take it out, believe implicitly in its power. Remember too, that you can only use it once, for it will return to me when it has done your bidding. Take it with my blessing.'

Merryn held out her hand for the silken bag. To her surprise, as soon as she grasped it, The Fairy Woman and her Elders disappeared.

'Wow!' said Jake. 'If I hadn't seen it with my own eyes I wouldn't believe it.'

'You'd have a job to see it with anyone else's eyes,' Hamish joked, 'but I know what you mean. Magic is hard to understand. You never know what's going to happen next.'

'Well I hope it's Travel Magic,' said Peter. 'My tummy's rumbling. I'm ready for my tea.'

Merryn held out her hands and they formed their inward-facing circle.

'Back,' she said, and there they were—and time hadn't moved on by a single second.

When midnight struck, the scene at McCaig's Tower was a very different one. The Grand High Witch had summoned every single witch. Ever since she had eliminated Mandragora Twitch she had developed the most terrible temper. She was angry with herself for acting too quickly, for failing to discover why Mandragora had been unable to capture Emily. Someone must be protecting the child. That was obvious, but who? If she'd had a little patience she could have made Mandragora tell her. Now it was too late.

But it wasn't too late to turn her anger on the other witches. She couldn't forget how they'd chanted Mandragora's name and she would never forgive them. She had ruled them for centuries and she was determined to go on ruling them for ever. She wasn't going to admit that Mandragora was right, that without The Snake Wand she was practically powerless. The remaining witches must never discover her true identity, or how she'd stolen The Snake Wand's secret and cheated her way into becoming The Grand High Witch.

'From now on,' she said as she stood before the assembled witches, 'my word is Law. I hereby abolish The Grand High Council.'

The sudden shocked silence was broken by words of protest and murmurs of disbelief. As a dozen brave witches stood up to argue The Snake Wand raised its ugly head. It flashed and flickered and darted from one to the other, and within the space of a single second they had all been eliminated. Behind The Grand High Witch the members of The Grand High Council huddled together. Without exception they belonged to The Wand Clan, and now they took out their wands and pointed them at The Grand High Witch.

One of them took a tentative step forward. 'You are making a dreadful mistake,' she said. 'Our strength lies in the number of Members of The Gr...'

The Grand High Witch whipped round. The Snake Wand darted. Its deadly venom flew to the witch who had spoken—and she too was gone.

The remaining members of The Grand High Council tip-toed back to their chairs in silence. In the hall, below the great dome, the other witches panicked. They pushed and pulled one another, climbed over seats and tried to get away. But before any of them could leave, The Grand High Witch raised The Snake Wand again.

'Flight is impossible,' she shouted. 'I have bolted the doors and barred the windows. Go back to your seats and sit in silence until I decide what to do with you.'

The only sounds in the great hall were of shuffling feet, rustling cloaks and stifled sobs. Pale-faced witches hung their heads as they avoided the terrible red eyes of The Snake Wand. When all was quiet, The Grand High Witch paced backwards and forwards across the stage. The click-clack of her boots broke the ominous silence. The Snake Wand writhed this way and that as it searched the audience for signs of movement. Time passed. The witches sat in fear and trembling, each one wondering if this day would be her last. Still The Grand High Witch's boots clicked and clacked from one side of the stage to the other. Eventually she stopped and thrust The Snake Wand into the air above her head.

'My decision is made,' she cried. 'No-one leaves this room until they have sworn allegiance to me. Anyone who refuses, anyone found guilty of disloyalty or treachery will be publicly eliminated.'

'I refuse,' cried the young witch whose grandmother had been eliminated. 'I would rather die than bow down to you.'

'Then die!' The Grand High Witch screeched.

The Snake Wand darted its head. Its forked tongue flicked out, its red eyes flashed and the young witch vanished.

'Raise your hand if you wish to follow her,' said The Grand High Witch.

No hands were raised. No voices called in protest. The Grand High Witch smiled a triumphant smile.

'One by one, you will kneel before me and promise to obey me in all things at all times. We will begin with the former members of The Grand High Council.'

She sat on her throne-like chair and called the first witch to step forward.

'Kneel,' she commanded. 'Kneel and make your promise.'

The terrified witch could barely speak but she managed to whisper the words. 'I promise to obey you in all things at all times.'

'Now,' said The Grand High Witch, 'raise your left hand.'

As soon as the witch had done so, The Snake Wand's tongue darted out and pierced her palm. A gasp from the audience was drowned by a yell of pain.

'Wimp,' shouted The Grand High Witch. 'You're not permanently injured, just marked for life. Two little red spots to remind you that you must always do my bidding.'

One by one, the other witches were forced to submit to the same treatment. Not until the last one had completed the ordeal, did The Grand High Witch give a full explanation.

'From this day forward, your power has been transferred to me. You are servants of The Snake Wand. The seeds of his power have been sown in your palms and you can do nothing without his knowledge. If I thrive and The Snake Wand thrives you will thrive too, but be warned, if we are overpowered, you will be overpowered too. It is therefore in your interest to do all you can to protect us.'

Chapter 23

'I think our search should start with Fairy Folk,' said Merryn. 'I've been reading about them and one of their favourite places is near Aberfoyle. I think we should go there now.'

Eager to continue their search for The Grand High Witch's name, they formed their circle and Merryn called out their destination.

'The Fairy Knowe, Doone Hill, Aberfoyle.'

Oban was left behind and they found themselves on a carpet of pine needles in a clearing in a hilltop wood. For a few minutes their quest was forgotten as they looked up at the huge Scot's Pine tree with its cone-laden branches. But it was the trunk that really caught their attention. Ropes had been wound around it and were hung with ribbons, hearts, necklaces and a single, lonely teddy bear. Scraps of fabric in a range of bright colours, bracelets, key-rings and hand-written messages covered the gnarled bark. Bunches of flowers and models of tiny fairies lay at the foot of the tree. More ribbons dangled from the lowest branches, and the trees round the edges of the clearing were festooned in the same way.

'What are all these things for?' asked Rosie.

'They're wishes,' said Merryn. 'There was a man called Robert Kirk. He used to come here to talk to The Fairy Folk and he wrote a book about them. That was more than three hundred years ago and ever since then people have come to visit. They leave gifts on the tree in the hopes that the fairies will make their wishes come true.'

'I suppose it's a bit like leaving coins in a wishing well,' said Emily.

'And that's a waste of money,' said James. 'Wishes don't come true. Things either happen or they don't and wishing doesn't make any difference.'

'Don't say that,' said Rosie, 'I like the idea of wishes and so do lots of other people.' She pointed to the evidence. 'Hundreds of people have made wishes and if I'd brought something special I'd make a wish too.'

'Anything will do, as long as your wish comes from the heart.'

'But you still can't guarantee that it'll come true.' James stopped and looked round. 'Who said that?'

'None of us,' said Merryn. 'It was a Fairy.'

'Indeed it was. I am a true Fairy and my name is Serena.'

They turned as a figure in a long green dress stepped out of the trees. She was nothing like The Fairy Woman of Tiree. She was young and beautiful with hair that fell to her waist in golden curls, but the expression on her face was stern and serious.

'I stand by what I said although what the boy says is partly true. We do our best, but sometimes it is wrong to interfere with destiny. Besides, there are some wishes that should never come true.'

'Why?' Peter asked.

'Because not all wishes are honourable,' said Serena. 'Those that are born of greed or hatred, and those that aim to harm others do not deserve to come true. And remember this, wishes alone cannot control the future. If you really want something you must do more than wish. You must strive to make it happen for yourself.'

'That's what we're doing' said Merryn, 'but you've confused me. We want to destroy The Grand High Witch. Surely that can't be wrong.'

'It's not,' said Jake, 'it's to stop her from destroying everything else.'

Serena gave a sad smile. 'Conflict, conflict, there is always conflict. What happened to peace and harmony?'

She looked at Merryn. 'I do not know enough about you to make a judgement. Tell me who you are and what you seek.'

Merryn stepped forward. 'I am Merryn MacQueen and these are my friends. Our quest is to rid the world of Malevolent Witchery, but in order to do so we need The Grand High Witch's true name. Can you help us?'

Serena shook her head. 'I do not know the name you seek. Even if I did, I would not tell you. Mortal children should not be embarking on such a dangerous mission. I can tell you have magical powers by the way you arrived, but I do not know if they are for good or ill. All I know of The Grand High Witch is that you would be wise to keep away from her.'

'We can't,' said Jake. 'Merryn and I have The Gift and we're honour-bound to join the fight against her.'

'Interesting,' said Serena, 'but how can I be sure that you are speaking the truth? You have arrived out of the blue and for all I know you may be trying to overthrow my people.'

'Oh! For goodness sake,' Hamish spluttered. 'Do we look as if we're working for witches? The Benevolent Wizards are our friends. We're helping them.'

He pulled out his crystal and told the others to do the same. The light from them shone out, brightening the glade beneath the trees and focusing on the fairy.

Serena didn't flinch or hide her eyes. 'I can see your amethyst crystals,' she said. 'I know that their power comes from The Benevolent Wizards so I believe that you are speaking the truth.'

'If you don't know The Grand High Witch's name, can you help in other ways?' Merryn asked. 'When the time comes to do battle with The Malevolent Witches, will you and your people join us? And if you can't, can you give us a Token that will add to our power? The Fairy Folk of Fang an t-Sithein on Tiree have pledged their support. The Fairy Woman gave us the heart-stone.'

'Did she indeed?' Serena raised her eyebrows in surprise. 'That is not what I expected to hear.'

'It was a surprise to me too,' said Merryn, 'but she trusts us to use it well. She loaned it to us once before. We used it to stop The Witch of Tiree from waging war on her and her people.'

'Then you are brave and I admire your determination. If The Fairy Folk of Tiree have pledged their support then I will pledge mine too.'

She pointed to the offerings that hung from the trees. 'Each one of those is a wish, an indication of the troubles of the world. We try to make them come true, but by joining in your quest, we may do even greater good. My people will help you, but how will you call us when we are needed?'

'I...I don't know,' Merryn stammered. 'We get in touch with the wizards through our crystals. We have a special shell for contacting Sula, The Selkie, but I don't know how to contact anyone else. Can you help us to find a way?'

'I believe I can,' said Serena, 'but you should have thought of that before you set out. You must plan more carefully. Nothing must be left to chance. Facing The Malevolent Witches is neither for the unprepared nor for the faint-hearted.'

'We're not faint-hearted,' Hamish protested. 'We're brave, all of us. We've already put an end to two witches and we've helped The Benevolent Wizards to trap The Clickfinger Locket.'

Merryn began to apologise for Hamish's interruption, but Serena waved her hand as if it was of no importance.

'I admire the boy for speaking out,' she said. 'And now that I know something of your previous conquests I am even more determined to help you.'

She lifted her hand and plucked something from the air.

'Take this miniature Silver Chanter,' she said. 'When the time comes to do battle, when all our combined forces are needed, you must blow it seven times. All those who have pledged their support will hear it. They will know where you are and they will come to your aid. There is no need for you to visit every Fairy Knowe. I will send out my messengers and do that for you. Every Fairy Company in Scotland will be ready and waiting for your call. In the meantime you must concentrate on recruiting other magical beings to your cause.'

Merryn held out her hand for The Silver Chanter, but Serena stopped her.

'Not so fast,' she said. 'Guard it well. Do not blow it until it is time for the battle to commence. And yet,' she paced up and down as if she was trying to make a decision, 'and yet, it may be needed before the final battle. Keep an open mind because in the world…'

The children joined in with the words that Serena had started to say.

'… of magic anything is possible.'

Serena smiled. 'You have learned your lesson well. You are on the side of all that is good and I will be proud to fight beside you. Now, I suggest that you seek The Ghillie Dubh. He lives in the highlands near Loch a Druing in the Gairloch. I believe he has a Token that will help you, but do not ask for it. Tread softly and wait for him to make an offer.'

Chapter 24

The seven children touched down on a carpet of moss in the shade of birch trees at the edge of Loch a Druing. A robin cocked its head and flew off in a flutter of wings. When it returned it was perched on the finger of a tall dark-haired man.

If the bird hadn't so obviously trusted him, they would have backed away in fear, for the figure that stood before them was wild and unkempt. His black hair hung in tangles around his shoulders and he was wearing nothing but a rough tunic fashioned from leaves, moss and woven grasses.

'I am The Ghillie Dubh,' he said in a voice that was low and gentle. 'I am of The Fairy Folk, but unlike them I live alone. I am The Guardian of the Trees and the woods are my world. I heard of your quest and I will help you because I too wish to end Malevolent Witchery.'

Merryn took the hand that he offered. 'I am Merryn and this is Jake. We both have The Gift and are honour-bound to fight all that is evil. This is my brother Hamish. The girls are Emily and Rosie, and the boys are James and Peter. The Benevolent Wizards gave us the power of Travel Magic so that we could help them.'

'I am pleased to meet you,' said The Ghillie Dubh.

'How did you hear about us?' asked James.

'News came on a breath of breeze and in the ripple of water,' said The Ghillie Dubh. 'Words are not needed for those who know how to listen. I know that you seek the true name of The Grand High Witch. I do not know it, but I have another way of helping you. Come with me. I have something that will prove invaluable.'

For several minutes he led them down woodland pathways where sunlight made dappled patterns at their feet.

'Here we are,' he said at last. 'Come inside and welcome.'

Although they looked round they couldn't see a door of any kind. Laughing softly at their puzzled faces he pushed aside a curtain of trailing honeysuckle. They ducked beneath it and stopped enthralled, speechless with delight.

Rosie was the first to break the silence. 'It's perfect,' she whispered, 'absolutely perfect. Look at the walls, all hung with leaves and flowers.'

'And the furniture,' said Peter, 'made of logs and twigs, not sawn in bits and polished like at home.'

'Do you live here all the time?' Emily asked. 'And where do you get your food?'

'I do indeed. This is my home. I eat what I find in the woods—nuts and berries, seeds, leaves, flowers, roots and honey from the wild bees.'

'All by yourself,' said James. 'Don't you get lonely?'

'Never,' said The Ghillie Dubh. 'I have birds and other creatures for company.'

He picked up a handful of hazel nuts and jiggled them in his hand. A squirrel appeared in the doorway, chittering excitedly. It leapt onto The Ghillie Dubh's arm, helped itself to a nut and scrambled back the way it had come.

'Wow,' said Merryn. 'That's brilliant, but I'm sorry. We shouldn't be asking so many questions.'

'I do not mind,' said The Ghillie Dubh. 'They are intelligent questions and company like yours is good, but I must not delay you. Your quest is urgent and I must help you on your way. I have few possessions and The Flint Arrowhead is my only treasure. I found it when I was digging for roots. At first I did not like it for I knew it had been fashioned for killing, but I washed away its encounters with death and gave it a peaceful purpose. If you are ever in need of help, lay it on a flat surface. Allow it to spin and it will guide you.'

He placed it in Merryn's hand. 'Take good care of it, and if you can, return it to me when you have achieved your goal. As for the name you seek, a visit to The Urisk in Glen Orchy may be fruitful. And now, may I see how your Travel Magic works?'

'Of course,' said Merryn.

The children crossed their arms and joined hands in an inward facing circle. Before she spoke the word that took them home, she thanked The Ghillie Dubh for his help.

He waved farewell and said, 'Remember, if in doubt it will show the way.'

'We won't forget,' said Jake.

'Back,' said Merryn, and The Ghillie Dubh in his magical woodland home was left behind.

'There's no point in waiting,' said Jake when they touched down in Oban. 'Let's reverse the ring and head straight to Glen Orchy.'

They all agreed that it was a good idea, and after the usual ritual they found themselves on a footbridge overlooking a river. Downstream the water widened and flowed slowly between wooded banks. Upstream it forced its way through rocks in a tumble of small waterfalls. They leaned on the wooden handrail and peered into the foaming water.

'What exactly are we looking for?' asked Rosie.

'An Urisk,' said James, 'whatever an Urisk might be.'

'Oi!' An indignant voice came from the rocks in the middle of the river. 'What's an Urisk indeed? An Urisk is, well, um, er, it's an Urisk. It's what I am and that's it and all about it.'

'Come out and show us what you look like,' Hamish called. 'We've come specially to see you. The Ghillie Dubh said you might be able to help us.'

'Friends of The Ghillie Dubh are friends of mine,' said the creature as he leapt from a small dark cavern at the foot of a tiny waterfall.

'Here I am. This is what an Urisk looks like, but I am not just any old Urisk. I am The Urisk, The Chief of The Urisk Clan. Now what do you think of that?'

'Amazing,' said Merryn as The Urisk bounded from one rock to another on hairy goat-like legs.

'Are you a goat or a man?' asked Jake. 'I mean it's hard to tell. You seem to be a bit of both if you ask me.'

'I'm not asking you,' said The Urisk. 'I'm telling you. I am The Urisk. I have hooves and strong legs so I can leap about. I have a head and arms so I can, well, so I can do everything else.'

He took off his broad blue bonnet and the yellow hair that had been tucked inside fell down to his shoulders. He bowed low and tapped a pair of curved horns that sprouted from the top of his head.

'As for these, I'm not sure of their purpose. I suppose I could butt someone if I really wanted to, but I'm a peace-loving kind of chap and I've never tried. So they're useless really, except for decoration. I guess they go with the legs though.' He broke into peals of laughter and gave another low bow.

'The Urisk at your service,' he said. 'I am delighted to make your acquaintance and I will help you if I can.'

'Then tell us the true name of The Grand High Witch,' said Jake.

The Urisk turned pale and shuddered. He put his finger to his lips and dropped his voice to a whisper. 'It's better not to mention her. She gives me the heeby-jeebies and you never know who's listening.'

He leapt up onto the bridge, balanced on the handrail and looked up and down the river. He beckoned to them to come closer. He slipped something into Jake's pocket and whispered in his ear. Then he turned to the others. 'You'd better head home,' he said, 'lickety split and no messing. If she catches you asking questions like that you'll be... well, I don't like to tell you what you'll be. So be off with you.'

He waved his hand and in half a dozen bounds he had disappeared into the cave behind the waterfall.

'What did he say?' asked Hamish.

'I'll tell you when we get back,' said Jake. 'Quick, let's go.'

He pulled the others into their circle, and Merryn, sensing his anxiety, took them swiftly back to Oban.

'Come on,' said Hamish when they were safely back in McCaig's Tower. 'Tell us what The Urisk was talking about.'

'A Malevolent Water Witch,' said Jake. 'He's seen her swimming in the river.'

'I thought witches never bathed,' said Emily. 'Clickfinger said they were scared of water.'

'Water Witches are different,' said Jake. 'They're really good swimmers. The Urisk said she has webbed feet and skin like a frog. He said if she heard us plotting against The Grand High Witch she'd be after us. And if she knew he'd helped us, she'd be after him too.'

'Is that all?' Merryn asked. 'No Token?'

Jake pushed his hand into his pocket and pulled out a small ruby-red bottle decorated with green leaves and blue forget-me-not flowers.

'It's very pretty,' said Merryn, 'but what's it for?'

'He didn't say.' Jake flipped the golden lid and looked inside. 'It's empty so I've no idea what to do with it.'

Merryn put it in her pocket alongside the miniature Silver Chanter. 'I expect we'll find out, but didn't he say anything else?'

'Two things,' said Jake. 'He said we should visit The Selkie next, and best of all, he thinks The Grand High Witch's first name begins with B.'

Chapter 25

'Where shall we go to see the Selkie?' Merryn asked. 'Last time, I met him on Tiree, but we don't have to go there. I can throw the shell into the sea from anywhere. I don't know how he does it, but he said he'd meet me, wherever I am.'

'If we can choose,' said Rosie, 'let's go to Colonsay. I can show you where I live and Kiloran Bay is the best beach in the entire world.'

'That's fine with me,' said Merryn. 'If the rest of you are happy, Colonsay it is.'

Moments later they found themselves on a curve of golden sand between two rocky headlands. On one side lay the dunes. On the other, the Atlantic Ocean stretched away to the distant horizon. Merryn opened the sea-bean box, took out the Selkie's charm and returned the box to her pocket.

'Let's have a look at it,' said Jake.

Merryn put the tiny purple-tinged shell into his hand. He turned it over and over. He breathed in the salty tang of the sea—scents of seaweed, fish and the tarry smell of ropes. He held it to his ear and listened to the sounds of the sea that came out of it—the roar of waves, the rumble of shingle, the crying of gulls and the singing of seals.

'Last time I called Roane,' said Merryn, 'I had to find my way to the sea in the thickest fog I'd ever seen. I was on my own. I had to ask for a crystal pendulum and I'd no idea what to expect. I was terrified. The sea was rough. A huge wave knocked me over and I thought I was going to drown. It'll be easier today, with the sun shining, the sea calm and all of you here to help me.'

She took the shell from Jake and ran down the beach into the water. She called Roane's name, but there was no answer. She waded until the sea reached her armpits and then she stopped and called again.

'Roane, please answer. I need your help.'

A whisper reached her ears. 'I am no longer able to travel. Sula, my son will come if you throw the charm.'

She lifted the shell high above her head and hurled it. It twirled through the air in a ray of purple light and when it hit the water it sent out ring after ring of purple ripples. A sudden mist descended and out of it came Sula. A cloak of mottled sealskin covered his shoulders and his tendrils of damp hair curled like waves of the sea. The other children gasped in wonder, but Merryn showed no surprise for she had seen a Selkie before. Full of concern for Roane she forgot to give a formal greeting.

'Your father?' she asked. 'How is he?'

Sula shook his head. 'He is old and weak and it is time for me to take over as head of our family.'

'Please give him my love and tell him...' She sniffed. Her eyes filled with tears and she struggled to go on. 'Tell him I'll never forget him. I only met him once, but we shared stories and he told me about my great-great-great-great grandmother.'

'I know that story,' said Sula, 'and I am honoured to meet the second Merryn MacQueen. But tell me, why did you call him and what can I do to help?'

'Come and sit with me, meet my friends and I'll explain,' she said.

'First I must return the shell, for one day, you may need it again,' said Sula.

'Thank you.' Merryn opened the sea-bean box ready to pop the shell inside, but Sula stopped her.

'Ah!' he said. 'I know of this but I have never seen it. May I look?'

As he read the inscription his face broke into a smile. 'For Merryn MacQueen. Forever grateful — Roane, 1881'. She saved his life. Without her kindness he would not have returned to the sea. He would not have met my mother and I would not have been born. So I too have cause to be grateful. That is why I will always answer your call.'

He put the shell inside the box and handed it back to her. They crossed the beach together and he greeted the others before sitting beside them on rocks that rose above the sand. He listened patiently while Merryn told him about their quest to rid the world of Malevolent Witchery.

'Yours is an honourable intention,' he said, 'and although I cannot tell you the name of The Grand High Witch, I can help in other ways. We will fight at your side if the need arises and I will send a Token to help you.'

He stood up to leave, embraced Merryn and took Jake by the hand. 'This is a task for you,' he said, 'but you must prove yourself worthy even though you are the seventh son of a seventh son.'

Jake looked up in surprise. 'How do you know? I didn't know it myself until a week ago.'

'There is an aura about you,' said Sula. 'Watch carefully. When I disappear into the sea, begin to count the waves as they break on the shore. Count in sets of seven. The seventh wave of the seventh set will bring a Token with it. Catch it before the next wave drags it back. You must not fail for you will not get a second chance.'

Jake's fingers trembled at the thought of such a huge responsibility. He glanced at the others. They were relying on him and he mustn't let them down. He followed Sula to the sea's edge. He watched as the water rose up Sula's legs, reached his hips, his waist, his shoulders. When it finally covered the Selkie's head, he began to count the waves.

'Seven,' he called and he folded his thumb over his palm so that he could keep a tally. 'Seven,' he called as his first finger joined his thumb.

A ray of sun set the waves sparkling making it difficult to see where one wave ended and another began. 'Seven,' he cried. His second finger joined the others, but his chest tightened with anxiety in case he'd made a mistake.

'Seven.' He folded his third finger over his palm.

He wanted to pause, to close his eyes against the brightness, but he forced them open and went on counting. His eyes started to water, making it difficult to see with certainty. He wiped them on his sleeve.

'Seven.' His little finger joined the others.

He'd noticed that the seventh wave was always larger than the rest and now there were only two sets to go.

'Seven.' His eyes ached from dazzle and concentration. The sea took on a purple hue. He counted out loud as each wave rolled and broke.

'One... two... three... four... five... six...'

The seventh wave was the largest yet. It rose in a great crest and a sudden gust of wind sent spindrift flying. He held his breath as he waited for the crash. The wave paused for a moment, and as it broke it travelled up the beach in a tumble of bubbling white water.

'Seven.'

He blinked and stared, but where should he look? Would the Token land at his feet or should he search from side to side? Panic set his heart thudding as the next wave began its journey towards the shore. He'd almost lost hope, when, at the very last moment, a glimmer of silver slid back on the outgoing wave. He flung himself head first into the surf as the next wave rose above him.

The others ran down to meet him.

'Well,' Hamish shouted, 'did you get it?'

Jake rolled over and sat up. Another wave broke over him so that he spluttered and spat out a mouthful of salty seawater. He stood up laughing delightedly and he stepped out of the sea with a heart-shaped purse in his hand.

'Of course I did,' he grinned. 'Look, it's covered in silver sequins. They're like magical fish scales.'

'But what's inside?' asked Merryn.

They sat on the sand as Jake unzipped the purse and tipped two perfect pearls into Merryn's cupped hands. With great care he put them back in the purse and slipped it into his pocket.

'I got them so I'll take care of them,' he said. 'I haven't a clue what they're for, but I expect we'll find out.'

As they started to form their inward-facing circle, Sula's voice rose above the sound of the sea.

'Go to the Liddel Water and seek the Shellycoat. He may know the answer to your question.'

'Shellycoat!' Hamish exclaimed. 'What on earth's a Shellycoat?'

'It sounds like a tortoise or a turtle,' said Emily,' but we don't get either in Scotland.'

'And where's the Liddel Water?' Peter asked.

'I've no idea,' said Merryn, 'but let's get back to Oban, then the Travel Magic can show us.'

Chapter 26

The seven children leaned on the parapet of an old stone bridge above the Liddel Water. They looked down on a tree-lined gorge and watched swirls of foam making patterns in the water below.

'If Shellycoats live in the river we're stumped,' said Hamish. 'We can't get down there. The slope's too steep. It's impossible.'

'Maybe it lives under the bridge,' said Peter, 'and if it does it'll be some sort of troll.'

'I hope not,' Emily gasped. 'I definitely don't want to meet a troll.'

Hamish, thrilled at the thought of trolls, marched across the bridge, stamping his feet and chanting in a gruff voice.

'Fol-de-rol, I'm a troll and I'm going to eat you for my dinner.'

'Stop it,' said Emily. 'You're scaring me and if Shellycoats aren't trolls you're probably scaring them too.'

Completely ignoring her, Hamish carried on with his troll impression. 'Fol-de-rol, I'm a troll and I'm going to...'

A sudden scream made them dash across the narrow road to the parapet on the other side of the bridge. Farther up the river, in among a tumble of boulders, someone was thrashing about in the water.

'See, I told you.' said Emily. 'I bet that's a Shellycoat and you've scared it.'

The frightened cries suddenly changed to shouts for help. 'Save me, I can't swim.'

'It's not just scared,' said James. 'It's drowning.' He looked round in panic. 'We've got to save it, but how do we get down there?'

Merryn, who had been checking access to the river, had found a wooden stile that led down steps into a field on the other side of the bridge. 'It's this way.' she called. 'Quick. Follow me.'

She scrambled over the stile and ran alongside the river, crossing muddy cattle tracks, skirting round boulders and pools of water. The others followed, slithering through mud, hurrying to the water's edge, anxiously scanning the river for whoever was in trouble. They stopped close to the place where they'd seen signs of struggling, but there was no one in the water.

'Maybe we're too late,' said Hamish. 'Maybe he's already drowned or perhaps you just imagined it.'

'I didn't imagine it,' said Merryn. 'You didn't hear because you were too busy playing at trolls, but I definitely heard a call for help.'

She'd barely finished speaking when the cry came again.

'Help. I'm drowning.'

The shouts were moving rapidly down the river. Arms splashed frantically. A head disappeared, bobbed up and disappeared again. The children ran back the way they'd come. Peter threw off his trainers and was about to plunge into the river when James grabbed him.

'Don't. It's too dangerous,' he said. 'If you get carried away under the bridge we'll never get you out.'

Peter tried to break away, but James refused to let go. Hamish and Jake joined in. They clung onto Peter despite his kicks and struggles.

'Stop,' Merryn shouted. 'If anything happens to you it'll be terrible. We've got to stay together or we'll be stranded. Have you forgotten we can only use Travel Magic if there are seven of us?'

'Yes,' said James. 'If you get lost we'll all be lost. We've no idea where we are and we could be stuck out of normal time for ever.'

Peter stopped struggling and pushed the others away. 'OK,' he said, 'only we've got to do something.'

But the screams and cries for help had stopped. No arms flailed about and there was no sign of a head rising above the water.

'We're too late,' said Rosie with a sob. 'If that was a Shellycoat it must have drowned. I can't bear it.'

They stood in a huddle, staring in distress at the surface of the water. A moment later, a peal of high-pitched laughter rose above the ripple of the river. There, standing on the parapet of the bridge, shaking with merriment stood a most curious creature.

'It's a Shellycoat,' Jake whispered. 'It must be. It wasn't in trouble at all. It was just pretending.' He called out angrily. 'You rotten cheat, you made us think you were drowning.'

'Don't call me a cheat.' The creature shook its fist, leapt from the bridge and plunged into the river. There was a tremendous splash and although they watched and waited for several minutes, the creature didn't reappear.

James turned on Jake. 'Now look what you've done. You've made him cross. We'll probably never see him again.'

They all began talking at once, making suggestions and arguing about what to do next.

Merryn raised her voice above them all. 'That's enough. Just be quiet and leave it to me.'

She walked back upstream to a platform of bare rock that projected into the river. There she knelt down and looked into the deep water.

'If you're a Shellycoat,' she called, 'please come out. Sula, the Selkie told us to find you. He thought you'd be able to help us.'

After a minute or two, a trail of bubbles crossed the river towards her and a pale green face broke the surface.

'I am a Shellycoat and I am not a cheat,' said the creature, 'and I've only come because Sula sent you.'

He scowled at Jake through strands of straggly black hair. 'I don't like you. You shouted at me and you have no sense of humour. It was a game. It was a joke. It was supposed to be fun.'

'Well it wasn't,' said Jake.

'That's a matter of opinion,' said the Shellycoat. 'I thought it was hilarious.'

'It wasn't,' said Peter. 'I almost jumped in the river to save you. I would have too, if the others hadn't stopped me. What if I'd drowned?'

'Sorry,' said the Shellycoat. 'I didn't think anyone would care enough to try and save me. It was very kind of you and you wouldn't have drowned because I'd have saved you.'

Long bony fingers grasped the rocks as the Shellycoat pulled himself out of the river. There he stood, a strange squat creature, even shorter than Rosie. Skinny hands dangled from the sleeves of his long shell-covered coat and long bony feet poked from beneath the hem. He shook himself like a dog that's been swimming, and a great clattering drowned the sound of the river as hundreds of freshwater snail shells rattled and banged together. Droplets of river water splattered the children and they wrinkled their noses at the water-weedy smell that came with them.

The Shellycoat's face with its wide mouth, big flat nose and round, watery eyes tilted towards Merryn. 'What do you want to know? Hurry up. I haven't got all day.'

'We need to know the name of The Grand High Witch,' said Merryn, 'and we're hoping that you can tell us what it is.'

The Shellycoat sniffed and tapped his nose. 'That's for me to know and you to wonder.'

'Please,' Jake added. 'We need her name. It's really important. Sula was sure that you'd help us.'

The Shellycoat poked a finger at Jake. 'Well he was wrong and you'd better keep out of it. I don't like people who call me a cheat. In any case, The Grand High Witch never hurt me so why should I do anything to hurt her?'

'Because she's evil,' said Hamish. 'We have to get rid of her to save the world.'

'Rubbish,' said the Shellycoat. 'Don't exaggerate.'

'He's not exaggerating,' said Peter. 'It's true. She has a horrible Snake Wand and it kills people.' He clicked his fingers. 'Just like that. Poof—and they're gone.'

'And she tried to capture me,' said Emily. 'She was going to make me into her slave for ever.'

'Why should I believe you?' asked the Shellycoat. 'You're just a bunch of kids. Even if I told you The Grand High Witch's name you wouldn't be able to destroy her. She'd kill you as soon as she set eyes on you. I think you're playing tricks on me.'

He paused and scratched his head. 'In fact, I don't think Sula sent you at all. I reckon The Grand High Witch sent you. She's testing me to see whose side I'm on, and if I help you she'll be after me with The Snake Wand. Then it'll be like he said.' He nodded his head towards Peter and he clicked his fingers. 'Poof—and I'll be gone.'

'Don't be stupid,' said Jake. 'We're helping The Benevolent Wizards to fight the Malevolent Witches.'

'There you go again.' The Shellycoat poked his finger at Jake for the second time. 'Don't call me stupid, and if you think I'm going to listen to more insults you can think again.'

He turned away and his coat of shells clattered as he did a backward somersault into the river.

Chapter 27

All six children glared at Jake, and Merryn threw up her hands in exasperation.

'I know we need you, Jake,' she said, 'but I wish you'd think before you speak. Insulting people never helped anything.'

'He's not a person,' said Jake. 'He's a...a...'

'That's enough,' Merryn snapped. 'He's probably listening to everything we say. You'd better apologise.'

Jake pulled a face, but he turned to the river and called to the Shellycoat. 'I'm sorry if I hurt your feelings. I didn't mean to be rude. Please come back. We need to talk to you and we're not trying to trick you.'

They waited, watching the river for signs of the Shellycoat, but he didn't reappear.

'So, what do we do now?' asked James.

'Let me try to persuade him,' said Rosie.

'You can try,' said Jake, 'but it'll be a waste of time. I bet he doesn't know The Grand High Witch's name.'

There was a splutter of indignation from the other side of the river.

'Hush,' said Merryn in the faintest of whispers. 'He's listening. Go on, Rosie. See if you can make him change his mind.'

The others stepped away from the bank while Rosie knelt down and called the Shellycoat.

'Please come out,' she coaxed. 'We didn't mean to upset you. You frightened us. We really thought you'd drowned. Please talk to me. You don't need to speak to the others. I'll send them away where they can't hear. I promise.'

Once again, the Shellycoat's head emerged from the river. He pushed back his wet hair and a sly look crept over his face.

'All right, but before they go I want to ask something.' He looked up at Merryn. 'You said that Sula sent you. So, if you know about Selkie Folk you must know about things from the sea.'

Merryn nodded. 'Some things, but not very many.'

'What about little round things, creamy white and gleaming?'

'He means pearls,' said Peter. 'It's lucky we've got s...' He stopped as James nudged him with his elbow.

'Too late to shut him up,' laughed the Shellycoat. He jumped up and down in delight and his shells seemed to join in his laughter. 'He's given the game away. Pearls! That's what they're called. You've got pearls and I want some. Let's do a swap. The Grand High Witch's name in exchange for pearls.'

'No way, 'said Jake. 'You should help because it's the right thing to do. You shouldn't try to get something in return.'

The Shellyback spluttered indignantly. 'I told you to keep out of it. What I do is my business and it's nothing to do with a horrible rude boy like you.'

He turned his back and plunged into the river with a clatter and a splash.

'You've done it again,' Merryn yelled at Jake. 'What's wrong with you today? You've made things worse and there's no point in saying sorry when you obviously don't mean it.'

'Getting cross isn't helping,' said Emily. 'We have to decide what to do if he doesn't come back.'

'He will come back,' said Jake. 'He knows we've got pearls and he wants some.' His voice dropped to a whisper. 'Let's pretend we don't care.' His voice rose again. 'Forget him. Let's find someone else to help us.'

They put their heads together to discuss the options. They knew they'd have to make a deal, but they couldn't risk losing both pearls so early in their quest. They walked back the way they'd come, hoping that the Shellycoat would follow. But when they reached the stile, he still hadn't appeared.

'He's not coming,' said Hamish. 'We're well and truly stumped.'

'Let me try again,' said Rosie. 'He's lonely and I think he's cute. I love his shelly coat and I think we ought to be nice and patient with him.'

Jake snorted. 'Cute! Nice! Patient! I've lost my patience. If you think you can be patient, you go and try.'

'I will,' said Rosie, 'and you'd better stay here.'

She ran back to where she'd last seen the Shellycoat and she sat on a boulder at the water's edge.

'Mr Shellycoat, where are you? Please come and talk to me.'

Almost immediately the Shellycoat clambered out of the river, shook himself and sat down on a boulder beside her.

'I came because you called me cute,' he said. 'You're nice but I'm not keen on the others. I don't know whether to help or not, but tell me why you want The Grand High Witch's name and I'll think about it.'

'We already told you,' said Rosie. 'She wants to put an end to everything that's good. If we know her full name we'll have power over her and then we can destroy her.'

She looked anxiously into the Shellycoat's watery eyes. 'You do know her name, don't you?'

'Not all of it,' he admitted. 'I'll tell you her first name, but I won't do it for nothing.'

Rosie sighed. She'd hoped to go back to the others with all three names, but one would have to do for a start.

'I think it begins with B,' she said.

'Who told you that?' The Shellycoat's eyes opened wide in surprise.

'The Urisk,' she said. 'He'd have told us all of it if he hadn't forgotten.'

The Shellycoat stuck out his bottom lip and made a sulky face. 'It's all right for him,' he said, 'he has a fine blue bonnet and a stick of rowan wood. All I have are shells and I get tired of their clattering. I've never had anything to treasure and now's my chance. I'll tell you, but only if you give me some pearls.' He looked up at the slides that were holding Rosie's hair in place. 'And I'd like those things from your hair too.'

'You'll get one pearl—if you're lucky,' she said.

He opened his mouth to complain, but she stopped him with a wag of her finger. 'No arguing, and there's no need to be greedy. We only have two pearls and we have to keep one for emergencies. One is all we can spare and I can't even promise that. The others will have to agree. So wait here while I try to persuade them.'

She scrambled back to where the others were waiting. 'He wants pearls in exchange,' she said.

'You shouldn't have agreed,' Jake shouted.

'I didn't,' Rosie shouted back, 'and there's no need to get mad at me. I said it might be one pearl and that I had to ask you first.'

'We'll still have one pearl left,' said Merryn, 'and if we get all three names it'll be worth it.'

Rosie sighed. 'I'm afraid he's forgotten her surname, so it'll only be two, but surely, that's better than none. Let me take the pearl, please.'

There was a lot of arguing, but eventually Jake unzipped the purse and put a single pearl into her hand. A few minutes later she showed it to the Shellycoat. His eyes brightened, but as his long fingers reached out to snatch it, she quickly closed her fist.

'Tell me the names first,' she insisted.

'I'll tell you one,' said the Shellycoat, 'then I want the pearl. It's Bubonica.'

He held out his hand and she put the pearl into it. A look of wonder crept over his face as he gloated over it. It was as if he'd forgotten she was there.

Rosie tapped the shells on his shoulder. 'The second name,' she said.

He turned away and hung his head. He shuffled his bare feet and whispered. 'I...I wasn't exactly telling... the truth. I think I...I've forgotten it.'

Rosie drew in her breath. What should she do? The pearl for one name was a poor bargain and she dreaded telling Jake that she'd been tricked.

The Shellycoat glanced at her in a sideways sort of way and pointed to her hair slides. 'Maybe those'll jog my memory.'

She felt like shouting at him. Jake was right. The Shellycoat was a cheat. He wasn't being fair, but she knew that she'd have to be careful. Now he'd got his pearl he might jump into the river and disappear for good.

'There's no need to make another bargain,' she said. 'I was going to give them to you anyway.'

She unfastened the slides, leaned over and clipped back his hair. 'There you are,' she said. 'They're a present from me.'

His face took on a tinge of pink as if he was blushing. 'I've never had a present before,' he said. 'You make me ashamed of myself.'

'And so you should be,' said Rosie, 'but let's forget it. Tell me what you know and we'll call it quits.'

'I really have forgotten her second name,' he said, 'but it begins with a V and it rhymes with Bubonica. I don't know her surname either, but it's something to do with the way she makes magic.'

He sniffed and rubbed his eyes. 'I like you and I'm going to miss you, so if you're going, you'd better go. I hate long goodbyes.'

He got to his feet, stood on tiptoe, gave her a quick kiss on the cheek and plunged into the river.

Chapter 28

On Saturday morning, Jake and Rex went over to Kerrera. They wandered along the track with Merryn while they waited for Hamish to finish his homework.

'I've been trying to work out The Grand High Witch's second name,' said Jake. 'Bubonica V-something. Veronica's a flower so that's too nice. How about Vubonica?'

'No,' said Merryn, 'it doesn't mean anything. I checked the dictionary last night and I found a truly nasty word. It's Vomica. It means a disgusting sort of abscess full of pus. It's the perfect name for a witch.'

'Bubonica Vomica,' said Jake. 'It sounds right. But even if it is, we still need her surname, and we can only get that if we see her making magic without The Snake Wand.'

'And if we can see her, she'll be able to see us, and if she sees us she'll destroy us,' said Merryn.

'Exactly,' said Jake. 'So we need another plan.'

'But we still need her name,' said Merryn. 'We'll have to keep travelling and asking. On Monday when Rosie's back from Colonsay we'll go out again. There are other magical beings that might know. We could look for unicorns and elves, or even giants.'

She covered her mouth and whispered. 'Hush, someone's coming.'

They shielded their eyes against the sun as a man came towards them.

'I think it's a wizard,' Jake exclaimed. 'I wonder what he wants.'

'We'll soon find out,' said Merryn, 'and it isn't just a wizard. It's The Great Wizard himself. Whatever it is, it must be important.'

As soon as he reached them, The Great Wizard stretched out his arms and grasped their hands. 'Finding you together is fortunate indeed,' he said. 'We are urgently in need of your help. You must join me on a journey. I trust that you have your crystals and your Tokens.'

'Of course,' said Merryn, 'I never go anywhere without them.'

Jake patted the pocket of his jeans. 'I have mine too.'

'Good,' said The Great Wizard, 'because I must take you to The Land of Benevolent Wizardry.'

'But, you can't,' Merryn protested. 'Tobias said I couldn't visit your land because there's no way back. I can't leave mum and dad and Hamish and... and everything.'

'And I'm not leaving Rex,' said Jake, 'not for anything.'

'They will be here when you return,' said The Great Wizard. 'They will not notice your absence, and Tobias was not exactly right. He is unaware of Magic that is for my eyes alone. It is true that mortals have never returned from my country, but that is because mortals have never visited it. Come with me and I will do all in my power to see you safely home.'

'But your power might not be enough,' said Merryn. 'Can't we fight The Grand High Witch here?'

'Yes,' said Jake. 'We could hide behind the rocks. We could ambush her, take her by surprise.'

The Great Wizard sighed. 'If it was so simple we would have eliminated her long ago, but it will not do. I must return home and you must go with me, for only those with The Gift can save my son.'

A heavy weight seemed to drop into Merryn's stomach. 'Save Kester?' she gasped. 'Why? What's happened to him?'

'When he became a Full Wizard,' The Great Wizard explained, 'he set out to visit you, to thank you for saving his life. The Grand High Witch disguised herself as you. She tossed a stone to him, and when he caught it he knew that he had been tricked. He felt so unwell that he returned home without seeing you. As the days passed he grew cold and silent. On the tenth day after his return, everything he touched...'

At this point, The Great Wizard passed his hand over his eyes and struggled to continue. His voice shook and fell to a whisper. 'Everything he touched turned to stone. Food and water became stone. Four days later he too turned to stone.'

'No,' Merryn cried out in horror. 'Tell me it isn't true.'

'I wish with all my heart that I could,' said The Great Wizard, 'but I cannot. The Stone Spell is truly terrible. We did not know it at the time, but in the fourteen days before he turned to stone, the infection passed to everyone and everything he touched.'

Jake shrank back. 'And you expect us to come and touch him? '

'Fear not. The Stone Spell will not infect mortals. You will be safe, and because of The Gift you are the only ones who can help.'

He turned away and buried his face in his hands. 'My son,' he murmured, 'you must save my son.'

Merryn clenched her fists and screwed up her eyes in an effort to stop from crying. Imagining Kester as hard and silent as a statue filled her heart with an unbearable ache.

'I don't understand,' said Jake. 'How do you know about The Stone Spell if you weren't there? And if you were there, why weren't you turned to stone?'

'Tobias and I were away from home,' said The Great Wizard. 'Otherwise we too would have been infected. The information was transmitted to us. We were warned to stay away. Tobias returned home, but he isolated himself in The Lodge of The Portal. Our people were told not to visit him while he tried to find a cure. But even if he finds one, it will be useless without you and The Gift.'

Jake sighed and looked at Merryn. 'I suppose you believe him.'

'I do,' she said. 'I don't know why, but I know he's telling the truth. We were given The Gift for a reason and I think this is it. If The Benevolent Wizards disappear Malevolent Witchery will destroy our world. We have to help.' She touched The Great Wizard's arm. 'I'll come with you.'

The Great Wizard gave the ghost of a smile. 'Bless you, my child. Come, let us leave before The Grand High Witch finds me.'

He turned to Jake. 'If you join us you will fulfill your purpose, but the decision must be yours.'

Merryn opened her mouth to plead with Jake, but The Great Wizard shook his head. 'No, it must be his choice.'

As he spoke he put an arm round Merryn. 'On my own I can leave your world from anywhere and I can reach my homeland in an instant. With you, I must find a hilltop where the air is clear and no human habitation breaks the sky. Never before has a mortal made this journey and my progress will be slow, but I am determined to succeed.'

His long legs took great strides, and Merryn, struggling to keep up with him, ran at his side. They climbed upwards and she shivered as a sudden mist descended. She could see nothing in front and nothing behind. It was as if the entire island had disappeared.

'It is the power of Malevolent Witchery,' said The Great Wizard. 'The Grand High Witch is on our trail.'

'Wait.' Jake's voice came through the mist. 'I'm coming, but I can't see. Where are you?'

'Here,' called Merryn.

Minutes passed. The mist grew thicker. Shouts between Jake and Merryn sounded eerily through the gloom, but The Great Wizard didn't pause. By the time they reached the summit of Carn Breugach, Jake, gasping for breath, had managed to catch up with them.

The Great Wizard set Merryn astride his left hip and Jake astride his right hip. 'Hold one another's hands,' he said, 'with one pair in front of me and one pair behind me. That's right. Now we are ready.'

As they rose into the air Merryn felt something grasp her waist. She tried to shout a warning, but her words were carried away on the wind. A rush of icy air made her want to stuff her hands into her pockets, but she couldn't let go of Jake. And worse, far worse than the cold, was the fear of the thing that was travelling with them.

Up and on they went. Gradually, the sound of the wind died away to a whisper. She tried to tell The Great Wizard about the hands that were holding her, but he was so tall and she was so small that her face was pressed against his back and her voice was muffled. Then, the thing that was clinging to her, called her name.

'Merryn.'

Relief flooded through her as she recognised her brother's voice. 'Hold tight,' she gasped, 'and don't let go.'

'Merryn,' he called again. 'Someone's holding onto me. It's a woman. I think it's a witch.'

Merryn gasped. All the magic she and Jake possessed — her necklace, the crystals and the Tokens — all had failed to protect them. Even the power of The Great Wizard was proving useless. This was no ordinary witch. It must be the most powerful witch of all — The Grand High Witch herself.

As they sped through the air her mind raced over the choice she had to make. If she let go of Jake's hands they would fall to earth and be killed. If she didn't let go, The Grand High Witch would reach The Land of Benevolent Wizardry. There would be an almighty battle and if the witch won, it would be the end of them all. She had to take a chance. She couldn't let go. The moment they arrived she would warn The Great Wizard, and if all went well, he would win.

Chapter 29

As they continued their journey, Merryn sensed that
something was changing. The huge expanse of space
disappeared. Shapes loomed in front of them, and with
a sudden jolt they touched down in a narrow rock-
strewn valley.

'The Grand High Witch,' she yelled as she let go of
Jake's hands. 'She's followed us.'

The Great Wizard whipped round and pointed his
first finger.

The Grand High Witch backed away, still clutching
Hamish by the waist. 'Use your magic,' she snarled,
'and I'll kill him.'

'No,' Merryn screamed, 'let my brother go.'

The Great Wizard sent a thin sliver of magic to the
hands of The Grand High Witch.

'Argh,' she yelled as her hands flew apart.

Hamish took his chance, broke free and ran to
Merryn. Open-mouthed and overawed, the three
children watched The Grand High Witch's hands
jerking and jittering as she tried to shake off the
wizard's magic.

'Go.' The Great Wizard pushed them away. 'Stay
out of sight, you can do no good here.'

Merryn, with Jake and Hamish following, ran
towards a building that stood alone in the dreary grey
landscape. They dashed behind the wall and took
turns to peer round the corner to see what was
happening.

The Great Wizard pulled, not one, but two wands from the sleeve of his tunic. 'At last we meet in fair combat,' he said. 'Once and for all we will see whose magic is the stronger.'

'It's mine,' yelled The Grand High Witch as she dodged the spells that flew from The Great Wizard's wands. Gradually, her hands stopped shaking and when she finally gained control of herself, she strode confidently towards The Great Wizard. As if from nowhere, a thunderbolt flashed, hit his chest and hurled him backwards. She waved The Snake Wand above her head and venomous spells sped through the air. They collided with the spells from The Great Wizard's wands and, like exploding fireworks, they bounced off the rocks and bombarded the walls of the building.

'I can see you, you interfering brats,' she cried. 'Hide if you can, but when I've finished with The Great Wizard I'll finish you.'

The children drew back and looked at one another in dismay. She had noticed their hiding place and they could no longer peep out to see what was happening. Their only clues came from angry voices, cries of pain and the zap of magic on the surrounding cliffs.

'We can't show our faces again,' said Jake. 'We'd be dead in no time. How on earth can we help?'

'We can't,' said Merryn. 'We didn't come to fight The Grand High Witch. We've got to stay safe so that we can break the spell and save Kester.'

'But we can't stand back and let her win,' said Hamish. 'We've got to fight. Let's look inside the building. There may be something that'll help.'

Merryn read the words that were carved above the open door. 'The Lodge of the Portal. Brilliant! This is where Tobias is waiting for us.'

'Great,' said Hamish. 'He'll join the fight and two wizards are bound to be better than one.'

Merryn took a step towards the door, but as she did so, she stumbled in dismay. There was no sign of wood. The door, standing ajar, was made of cold, hard stone.

'It's true,' she gasped. 'Everything The Great Wizard said is true.'

'But it shouldn't have reached here,' said Jake. 'The other wizards were told to keep away. Tobias was supposed to find a cure while he waited for us to arrive.'

Hamish clung to Merryn's sleeve. 'What sort of cure?' he demanded. 'And what did The Great Wizard tell you?'

Merryn slumped to the ground. 'He told us that The Grand High Witch had infected Kester with a deadly disease. It's called The Stone Spell and everyone who catches it turns to stone. She let him escape because she knew he'd come home and infect his people.'

'Crumbs,' said Hamish, his eyes registering panic. 'What if…what if we catch it?' He looked round for a way to escape. 'We're trapped. We'll turn to stone and that…that'll be the end of us.'

'No,' Merryn insisted. 'It's a spell for wizards, not for mortals. It won't harm us. That's why Jake and I had to come. We're supposed to cure everyone.'

'That was the plan before The Grand High Witch arrived,' said Jake. 'Now I'm not so sure. We can only do the cure if we get rid of her first.'

Hamish groaned. He covered his face with his hands and let them slide slowly down his cheeks. When his eyes reappeared they were filled with tears. 'I've spoiled everything. I've been really stupid. I've brought The Grand High Witch and it's all gone wrong.'

'Maybe, maybe not.' Merryn clutched her chest to calm the frantic flutter of her heart. It was no use blaming Hamish. She tried to steady her voice. 'What's done is done,' she said. 'It's what happens next that matters. If The Great Wizard wins the battle we'll be all right.'

'And if he doesn't?' Hamish asked.

'I daren't think about it,' said Merryn, 'but I know one thing. It's no use standing here wondering. I'm scared of what we'll find inside, but we need to know.'

Cautiously she passed through the half-open door and stepped inside The Lodge of the Portal. Seeing a door turned to stone was one thing, what she saw in front of her took her breath away. Everything was made of stone. Desk and chairs, filing cabinets, books and papers, pens and pencils, the clock on the wall, the curtains at the window—even the windows were made of stone.

Worse, much, much worse was the sight of Tobias sitting at the desk. It was not the Tobias they knew. It was not Tobias with a kindly smile, twinkling blue eyes and a long beard. It was Tobias turned to stone. Her hand flew to her mouth, her lips trembled and she struggled to catch her breath.

'We're too late,' said Hamish, 'but I want to know what's happening outside.' He stuck his head round the door. There was nothing to see, but the sounds of battle were as fierce as ever. He turned back to the desk. 'They're still fighting,' he said, 'so let's see what we can find.'

'We won't find anything,' said Jake. 'There's nothing but stone.'

'But we're supposed to break the spell,' said Merryn, 'so we've got to try.'

She crossed the room and placed a hesitant hand on the wizard's shoulder. The cloak that should have felt soft to her touch was hard. His beard was stiff and unyielding. His stone fingers held a stone pen as if he was writing. She covered his hands with hers. Jake placed his hands on the wizard's shoulders. They waited for a whole minute, but nothing changed.

'Well,' Jake shrugged with disappointment. 'That didn't work. The Gift isn't enough. It has to be combined with a wizard's spell and Tobias hasn't made one.'

'Even if he has,' said Hamish, 'he can't tell us.'

He looked at the book that lay on the desk. 'If we could read his writing it might give us a clue.'

'Let's use our crystals,' Merryn urged. 'Suspend them above it. They may not help, but it's worth a try.'

As they took out their crystals, rays of light shone round the room, brightening the dark corners and emphasising the stone shapes, but they didn't change anything. Merryn looked at Tobias and began to cry. Tears streamed down her cheeks and dripped onto the stone page.

'Look,' said Jake. 'Marks are starting to show.'

'It looks like the writing in Kester's Book,' said Hamish, 'and your tears are uncovering it. Keep crying. You can't stop now.'

'I don't want to cry,' she sobbed. 'I want it to be over.'

'But don't you see?' said Jake. 'The Gift and the tears are working together.' As each tear fell, Jake touched it with his fingertip and wiped it across the page. More letters appeared and formed into words, and Merryn's tears kept falling. She wept because she couldn't bear to see Tobias looking like a statue. She wept at the thought of Kester turned to stone. She wept at the hopeless feeling that engulfed her. After many more tears a whole page of neat writing appeared. She dried her eyes, leaned over the wizard's stone shoulder and began to read. The page started with the end of a sentence. She tried to see what came before it, but it was impossible. The stone page would not turn back.

Chapter 30

The stone book lay open on the stone desk. Its stone pages would not turn, but the wizard's handwriting was now clearly visible. Merryn, Jake and Hamish read in silence.

...nothing I could do. Nothing any of us could do. The disease advanced like a deadly army. As each infected person walked the land, everything they touched turned to stone. The water they tried to drink and the food they tried to eat turned to stone. The chairs they sat on and the beds they tried to sleep on turned to stone. Husbands saw wives turn to stone. Women saw their children turn to stone. Children saw their parents, their friends and their pets turn to stone. To make matters worse, people caught the disease by touching those who had already turned to stone.

The elders met together, but one of them must already have been infected. They kept in touch with me, but eventually their messages stopped. Then I knew that I was the only one alive. I read every spell book that I could find. I worked and worked and tried to find a cure, but I was overcome by grief. I wanted to venture out to be with my family, but I had to remain here. I had promised to await the return of The Great Wizard with

Merryn and Jake. In this wide universe they are the only ones who possess The Gift. Without them we do not stand a chance.

Then I heard the sound of weeping and my heart filled with hope. Someone else was alive. But when I saw my youngest grandson, my joy was short-lived. He came, seeking me, crying his distress, telling me that everyone had turned to stone, telling me that he and I were the only ones alive. He was too young to understand. So what could I do? He ran towards me and before I realised what I was doing, I held him close and tried to soothe him. But it was already too late. He turned to stone in my arms. Then I knew that it was too late for me too. I had a few days before everything I touched began to turn to stone. I worked day and night, still hoping to find a cure, but it was not to be. So I wrote this account of all that had happened. Then my pen began to turn to stone and I could write no...

The words stopped abruptly. Merryn, Hamish and Jake stared in dismay.

'I've never read anything so sad,' Merryn whispered. 'I can't bear to think of it. All those people watching their loved ones turn to stone.'

Hamish shuddered. 'And knowing that it would happen to them. That must have been awful, waiting and wondering and getting hungrier and thirstier and... and not being able to do anything about it, and...'

'Don't,' said Merryn. 'Don't say another word. It's bad enough thinking about it. Putting it into words makes it seem even worse.'

'Besides,' said Jake, 'we need to forget it and concentrate on what to do next. If The Great Wizard wins he'll come looking for Tobias. If he touches him he'll turn to stone and that really will be the end of Benevolent Wizardry.'

'And of us,' said Hamish. 'He won't be able to send us home so he mustn't come in. We've got to stop him. I'm going outside to tell him.'

'Wait.' Merryn grabbed his arm. 'We need to think about this. If The Grand High Witch sees you, she'll destroy you and that won't help anything.'

Hamish tried to pull away, but she clung on and Jake blocked the doorway to stop him from getting past.

'Don't you see?' Hamish spluttered angrily. 'We've got to stop her. The Great Wizard has to win and we've got to help him. It's our only chance.'

'You're right,' said Jake, 'but what can we do?'

'I don't know,' said Hamish, 'but I'll think of something.'

'Well, rushing out there isn't the answer,' said Merryn. 'Let's see what we have to help us. We all have crystals.'

'And hag-stones,' said Jake. He dug his hand into the pocket of his jeans and brought out the hag-stone that Tobias had given him.

Merryn and Hamish did the same.

'We have Tokens,' said Merryn. 'The most powerful one of all is the heart-stone, but we can only use it once and we mustn't waste it.'

'No,' said Hamish. 'The Fairy Woman said you must leave it in the bag until our time of greatest need and this may not be it. Besides, it didn't stop the witch from hanging onto us, so perhaps it isn't powerful enough, after all.'

'That's what worries me,' said Merryn. 'Anyway, I expect it to tell me when the time comes to use it. When it was ready to fight The Witch of Tiree, it started to buzz. I'm hoping it'll do the same again.'

She placed The Silver Chanter on the desk. 'It's a shame about this. If we'd been back on earth we could have called the Fairy Folk, but I don't think it'll work here. They won't be able to get through The Portal.'

'But we got through it,' said Hamish, 'and so did The Grand High Witch.'

'Yes, but that's because it opened for The Great Wizard and we were all travelling with him,' said Jake. 'I agree with Merryn. The Silver Chanter isn't going to help.'

Hamish scowled. 'You're not always right,' he muttered, 'so if you don't mind, I'll look after it.'

Neither Merryn nor Jake objected as he picked it up and slipped it into his pocket.

Merryn held up The Flint Arrowhead. 'Remember this from The Gillie Dubh.'

'Yes,' said Hamish, 'he said if we were lost it would tell us which way to go.'

'But we're not lost,' said Jake, 'and that isn't what he said. His exact words were—if in doubt it will show the way.'

'Same thing,' said Hamish.

'Not quite,' said Merryn. 'It might show us something else that can help.'

She placed The Flint Arrowhead in a space on the desk. As soon as it touched the stone surface it took on a golden glow. It changed from gold to orange, until, picking up speed it turned to yellow. Faster and faster it went, so fast that it became nothing but a blur of bright white light. Then it gradually slowed and turned back through yellow, orange and gold until it was flint again.

'For once you were right,' said Hamish, 'but that doesn't mean you're right every time.'

He squatted down so that his eyes were in line with the arrowhead. 'Look,' he said. 'It's pointing to something on the third shelf.'

Merryn dashed across the room and looked at the higgledy-piggledy heap of stone shapes. She put out her hand and picked up a stone sphere.

'No,' said Hamish. 'Keep going. It's farther to the right.'

Merryn's hand hovered over the objects as she moved it along the shelf.

'Stop,' shouted Hamish. 'That's it. Pick that one up.'

'It's just a cube,' said Jake.

'Ouch!' Merryn squealed as the necklace gave a sudden jolt. 'I know what it is,' she cried. 'It's The Clickfinger Locket. The wizards trapped it in a box and Tobias said he'd take care of it. They were trying to make a spell to destroy it.'

'But they didn't manage it,' said Hamish. He jumped up and down with excitement. 'This is it, it could be the answer.'

Jake shook his head in puzzlement. 'I don't see how.'

'Clickfinger said she'd eliminate The Grand High Witch,' said Hamish. 'She didn't manage it, but all her hate is inside the locket.'

'And the strength of The Clickfinger Clan is inside it too,' Merryn added. 'It's terribly powerful.'

Hamish couldn't help butting in. 'I said they ought to trap it and they brought every single wizard to help. There were dozens of them and The Great Wizard said the words of the spell, but they still couldn't destroy it.'

'So I don't see how it can help now,' said Jake. 'I think you're forgetting it's turned to stone.'

'Maybe it isn't,' said Hamish. 'Maybe it's just the box that's turned to stone. The locket might be safe inside.'

'I'm sure it is,' said Merryn. 'My necklace jolted as soon as I touched it, so the locket must still have its power. We'll have to be careful because it hates us too. But if we can get it out, I think it'll be on our side. It might be exactly what we need to put an end to The Grand High Witch.'

Chapter 31

Hamish snatched the stone box from Merryn's hand. He pushed past her and dashed through the door. 'What are you waiting for?' he yelled.

Stop,' Merryn called as she raced after him. 'It's too risky.'

Up to now, the thick walls of The Lodge had deadened the battle sounds, but the noise that met them was so terrifying that Hamish did stop. He stopped so suddenly that Merryn and Jake both bumped into him. All three of them clutched one another as they stood listening, knowing that the battle was far from over. Knowing too, that it was raging close to The Lodge. Shrieks and hideous laughter came from The Grand High Witch while The Great Wizard's deeper voice called out in anger. All around were the sounds of spells colliding in mid-air. They ricocheted from boulders and overhanging cliffs, filling the air with smells of burning and the crackle of explosions.

Merryn pulled Hamish back and peered cautiously round the corner. She chewed nervously on her fingers as she watched The Great Wizard being driven closer and closer to their hiding place. She could see that The Grand High Witch had the upper hand, and that her magic was coming from the forked tongue of The Snake Wand. It came in the form of black lines that flew straight as arrows, but that wasn't all. Each one was followed by a small round thunderbolt that knocked The Great Wizard off balance. And before he could steady himself, The Snake Wand sent another volley of venom. The Great Wizard managed to avoid most of it, but when it scored a hit, he cried out in pain.

Not bearing to watch any more, Merryn stepped back and turned to Jake and Hamish. 'The thunderbolts don't come from The Snake Wand,' she said. 'If we can see how she sends them we'll know the name of her Clan. Then we can call her name and that will give us power over her. Watch her, but be careful, don't let her see you.'

'She isn't a 'Wand' and she isn't a 'Clickfinger' because she uses both hands to hold The Snake Wand,' said Hamish.

'Perhaps she's a 'Word',' said Merryn.

'No. She isn't a 'Word',' said Jake. 'She can't speak. She's too busy laughing that horrible laugh.'

'Then she must be using her face,' said Merryn. 'Watch carefully and see how she does it. Is she a 'Sniff' or a 'Twitch' or a 'Sneeze' or a…'

'She's a 'Wink',' shouted Hamish. 'She winks her left eye and it sends a thunderbolt.'

'He's right,' said Jake.

'Yes!' Merryn punched the air. 'That's it. Now we have it. Her name is Bubonica Vomica Wink. We can help The Great Wizard to win. Cross your fingers and watch this.'

Taking a deep breath she stepped away from the building. She was only just in time because at that moment one of The Great Wizard's wands was caught by The Snake Wand's deadly venom. It splintered, flew out of his hand and fell to the ground in a smatter of tiny pieces. He stumbled as he tried to make one wand do the work of two.

Merryn shouted at the top of her voice. 'Bubonica Vomica Wink.'

The Grand High Witch reeled, toppled backwards and dropped to the ground with a dazed expression on her face.

The Great Wizard's power was much reduced, but it didn't stop him from repeating Merryn's words. 'Bubonica Vomica Wink,' he cried.

He staggered, his energy almost spent. His one remaining wand was no match for The Snake Wand. He tried to stand but each time he got to his feet, his legs buckled.

Hamish and Jake added their voices to Merryn's. 'Bubonica Vomica Wink,' they called.

Their words hit the surrounding cliffs and bounced back as echoes. 'Onica, omica, ink, onica omica ink.'

The Great Wizard, weakened now, was no longer calling, but Merryn and the boys didn't stop. They shouted The Grand High Witch's true name over and over again and the echoes kept on bouncing back.

'Onica, omica, ink, onica, omica, ink.'

The Great Wizard dragged himself across to The Lodge and slipped round the corner where The Grand High Witch couldn't see him. Jake followed to see if he could do anything to help.

'No, my boy, ' said The Great Wizard. 'I am not finished yet, but I need a moment to catch my breath. Bring my brother, he will be inside The Lodge.'

'He isn't there,' said Jake. 'We've already looked.'

'Then victory depends on me alone,' The Great Wizard groaned. 'I fear we have already lost.'

Round the corner, Merryn and Hamish were still shouting. With each repetition of her name, The Grand

High Witch shuffled backwards on her bottom, but her name alone was not enough to eliminate her. Merryn paused to catch her breath and Hamish's voice grew hoarse. He stopped shouting and began to cough, and in that moment The Grand High Witch struggled to her feet, swung round and faced Merryn.

'You've gone too far,' she shrieked, 'I'll put an end to you and your interfering Gift.'

Before The Grand High Witch could point The Snake Wand at Merryn, Hamish raised his arm and threw the stone box. He held his breath, suddenly afraid that he'd done a foolish thing, that the stone box would miss its target. With all his might he willed it to score a hit.

The Grand High Witch gave a feeble laugh. 'Call that a throw,' she exclaimed. 'You're no match for The Snake Wand. You don't even have The Gift. You're nothing but a wimp.'

The stone box did not hit The Snake Wand. It flew past, missing its mark by a hand span. The Grand High Witch's laughter grew to a crescendo, but it stopped abruptly when the stone box turned in a sweeping curve. Hamish watched with delight as it began to whirl round The Grand High Witch's head. Soon the whirling was accompanied by a cracking sound. The stone box was disintegrating. Bits of stone scattered far and wide and out came The Clickfinger Locket. It danced in the air, its chain swinging and swaying, its owl eyes zapping The Snake Wand with ray after ray of powerful blue light.

The Grand High Witch's left eye winked crazily as she tried to hit the locket with thunderbolts. The Snake Wand writhed and spat in an effort to avoid The

Clickfinger Locket's spells. And then, most terrifying of all, came a voice from the dead—the voice of Ammonia Begonia Clickfinger.

'I said I'd eliminate you and now I keep my promise, but first I'll make you suffer. I said you'd be useless without The Snake Wand and now I'll prove it.'

Malicious laughter rose and fell as the locket circled The Grand High Witch's head. Faster and faster it spun. Louder and louder came Ammonia's laughter. Then an unexpected silence fell as The Clickfinger Locket backed away.

The Grand High Witch looked round and gave a scornful laugh. 'See,' she cried, 'you've given up. You're no match for me. With The Snake Wand I am invincible.'

'But without it, Bubonica Vomica Wink, you are nothing,' cried the voice of Ammonia Begonia Clickfinger.

With those words, The Clickfinger Locket turned. It flew unerringly to pierce the left eye of The Snake Wand. The link between the wand and The Grand High Witch was so strong that she too felt the blow. Her left eye spurted a stream of black blood and she cried out in pain and despair. It was a cry so dreadful that it chilled the hearts of Merryn and Hamish. They covered their ears, but they couldn't stop watching. And Jake and The Great Wizard came out from behind The Lodge of The Portal to join them.

Together they watched as The Grand High Witch struggled to hold onto The Snake Wand. It writhed in agony, blood poured from its left eye while the tip of its tail lashed frantically. It broke away from the witch's grasp and fell to the ground. Gradually the writhing slowed, until, with one desperate shudder, it stopped.

The Grand High Witch tore her hair and cursed. She bent down and grasped The Snake Wand, but it lay limp and useless in her hands. She raised her head and faced The Great Wizard.

'You cheat,' she cried. 'In fair and equal combat I would have won. Victory was in my grasp, but this was not a fair fight.' She pointed at the three children. 'Those interfering brats should not have been involved. They think they've brought an end to our battle, but it is not over yet.'

She screwed up her bruised and bleeding eye and tried to wink at Merryn. Nothing happened. No thunderbolt came to strike. 'Then I will curse you,' she said. 'No good will ever...'

The Great Wizard pointed his one remaining wand and the unfinished curse ended. A stream of continuous purple magic linked the space between the two enemies. With little to counteract it, The Grand High Witch was helpless. She stood bravely, trying her hardest to deflect the magic, but The Great Wizard held his wand steady.

'Bubonica Vomica Wink,' he cried.

From the surrounding cliffs came the echo, 'Onica, omica, ink.'

The Grand High Witch was weakening. She was staggering. She was growing faint. She was fading away, and in a very short time she vanished as if she'd never existed.

Chapter 32

The Great Wizard folded his arms around the three children. 'No words can express my gratitude,' he said. 'Without your help, my land and my people would have been lost for ever.'

He led them to where The Snake Wand sprawled. Next to it was the hat that had been as important to The Grand High Witch as a crown is to a Queen. Merryn stood in silence as The Great Wizard touched The Snake Wand with his own wand. She watched as it shrivelled away to nothing, and she saw the hat burst into flames and turn to ashes that drifted away on a breeze.

'What's this?' asked Jake as he bent to pick up a twisted disc of metal.

'Don't touch it.' The Great Wizard grabbed his arm and stopped him just in time. 'It's the remains of The Clickfinger Locket and it may still retain some of its power.

'Wow!' said Hamish. 'What happened to it?'

'The clash between the two great powers was too much for it,' said The Great Wizard. 'It will be much weakened, so now we should be able to destroy it. Take out your crystals and let their light focus on it.'

He pointed his wand at the damaged locket and the children did as he asked. Four purple beams settled on the one blue eye that was visible. Although the metal spat and spluttered, the crystals didn't falter. The owl's eye burst into flame. It burned with a clear blue light that grew darker and darker until it vanished in a puff of black smoke.

'But where's the other eye?' Merryn asked. 'We've got to find it.'

All four of them looked round, peering into the grey dust that lay on the floor of the valley.

'There.' The Great Wizard pointed to a tiny speck of blue. 'It must have fallen out when the metal twisted. Let us treat it in the same way.'

Once again the wand and the amethyst crystals focused. This time there was no resistance. Detached from the locket, the eye seemed to be powerless. A small black flame burned briefly and the eye was gone.

The Great Wizard pointed his wand at the remains of the locket and chain. 'By the power of all that is good and true,' he cried, 'rid the universe of The Clickfinger Locket for ever and ever.'

'Ever...ever,' came the echo.

The bronze disc glowed. The chain tried to pull the locket away from the wizard's spell, but the metal was already melting. With a sudden bright flare it was consumed. The flames ran down the chain and it too burned away to nothing.

'No Grand High Witch,' said Hamish, 'no Snake Wand and no Clickfinger Locket. Is that it? Have we won?'

'We've won this battle,' said Jake, 'but the other witches will be there when we get back home.' He frowned. 'I mean, if we get back.'

'You will get back,' said The Great Wizard, 'and when you do, you will find that every trace of Malevolent Witchery has disappeared.'

'That's impossible,' said Merryn. 'There were hundreds of witches. They can't all have gone.'

'But they have,' said The Great Wizard. 'When The Snake Wand branded them it transferred all their power to The Grand High Witch. It gave her strength beyond all imagining. She could not have created The Stone Spell without it, and she could not have broken through our protection to travel with us.'

'But that doesn't explain why the witches have disappeared,' said Merryn.

'The branding linked them to The Snake Wand for ever,' said The Great Wizard. 'When it perished they perished too. Your earth is now free of Malevolent Witchery.'

'Crumbs,' said Hamish. 'So when I threw The Clickfinger Locket I killed them all? Every single one?'

The Great Wizard smiled. 'No, my boy, it was not you. It was the power of The Locket.'

'Yes, but I thought of it and if I hadn't thrown it…'

'You are right,' said The Great Wizard. 'I must give credit where credit is due. It was your action that triggered the beginning of the end.'

Hamish's grin grew so wide that it almost reached from one ear to the other.

'Well done, brother,' said Merryn. 'You were brilliant, but it's not why we're here. We came to rescue Kester. We still have to break The Stone Spell.'

'Yes,' said Jake, 'and we don't know how to do it. We tried and it was impossible.'

'You tried!' The Great Wizard cried in astonishment. 'But you haven't yet seen the effects of The Stone Spell. No! I beg you. Do not tell me it reached The Lodge. Do not tell me that my brother Tobias has turned to stone.'

By the expressions on their faces he knew it was true and he began to run towards The Lodge.

'No,' the children cried in unison. They chased after him. They clung to his tunic, his arms and his hands, desperately trying to hold him back.

'Don't go inside,' Merryn shouted.

The Great Wizard stopped. 'If Tobias has been infected there will be no one left.'

'There isn't,' said Hamish. 'His grandson came. They both turned to stone.'

The Great Wizard gasped. 'Then I must read the Log Book to see if he found a cure.'

'The Log Book is turned to stone,' said Jake.

'Then I must see it for myself,' said 'The Great Wizard.

'Don't go inside,' Merryn begged. 'If you do you might be infected.'

'And you promised to send us home,' said Hamish. 'If you turn to stone we'll be stuck here for ever.'

The Great Wizard paused. 'I am sorry. I am too distraught to think clearly, but do not worry, I will take the utmost care.'

He passed through the half-open doorway and stood looking at Tobias. 'My brother,' he gasped. 'I cannot bear it.' He tottered and put out an arm to steady himself. His hand wavered and although he tried to stop it, it came to rest on his brother's stone shoulder.

Merryn screamed. Jake gasped and Hamish launched himself at The Great Wizard and pummelled him with his fists.

'You've spoiled everything,' he shouted, 'you should have listened to our warning.'

'I am truly sorry,' said The Great Wizard as he grasped Hamish's hands, 'but fighting will not help. Step back and let me think.'

He leaned against the wall and closed his eyes. Merryn stood watching him. Jake went to the door and looked out while Hamish, unable to keep still, paced round the room muttering angrily.

Eventually The Great Wizard opened his eyes. 'I must make a plan before my energy fails me,' he said. 'Ten days will pass before the things I touch turn to stone. Do what you can to break the spell, and if you have failed by the seventh day, return to me. If you leave it later than that I may not have the strength to send you home.'

He leaned over the Log Book and read the words that Tobias had written. When he finished he looked up in surprise.

'How can words be legible when the book is turned to stone? I do not understand.'

'I cried,' said Merryn. 'A tear fell on the page and a letter appeared. I couldn't stop crying and Jake spread my tears out. After a while we could read it all.'

The Great Wizard's face lit up with hope. 'It is the answer. I knew that The Gift alone would not be enough. I thought that one of the elements would be involved—earth, air, fire or water. I did not think it would be water because the spell was turning water into stone. You have proved otherwise.'

Merryn looked round the stone-filled room. 'Even if I cried for the rest of my life,' she said, 'I couldn't make enough tears.'

'No, you misunderstand,' said The Great Wizard. 'Even I do not understand, but maybe the cure lies in pure water carried by someone who has The Gift. Surely, somewhere in our vast land there is water that still flows free. The likeliest place is our greatest river. It runs out of a cavern on the slopes of our highest mountain and it tumbles down waterfalls to the valley below. It is so remote that I cannot believe The Stone Spell has reached it. You must venture out and find it.'

'But you must come with us,' said Jake.

'No,' said The Great Wizard. 'My strength will fail and soon I will be unfit to travel. I will stay here and try to find a cure and you must return in seven days.'

'But a week's a long time,' said Hamish, 'what are we going to eat and drink when everything's turned to stone?'

'If you stay in this land you will feel neither thirst nor hunger, but I know the enormity of what I am asking,' said The Great Wizard. 'I will send you home now if that is your wish.'

Merryn answered without hesitation. 'We can't let you down. We'll stay. Tell us which way to go and we'll come back as soon as we've broken the spell.'

'And if we can't break it,' said Jake, 'we'll come back in seven days.'

'Then,' said Hamish, 'you'd better keep your promise and send us home.'

Chapter 33

'I hoped that when The Grand High Witch died, The Stone Spell would die with her,' said The Great Wizard, 'but it was not to be. The future of my people now lies with the three of you.'

Merryn twisted her fingers together at the thought of such a huge responsibility. 'We'll do our best,' she said. 'I just hope it's enough.'

She took one last look at Tobias and picked up The Flint Arrowhead from the desk. It had helped once and she hoped beyond hope that it would help again. She slipped it carefully into her pocket and went out of The Lodge.

The Great Wizard led them a little way along the track and pointed down the valley. 'The way grows narrower before opening out into a great plain with a river running through it. You will see our city before you, but do not go that way.'

He paused and passed a weary hand over his brow. 'It was the most beautiful of cities in the most beautiful of lands. I cannot bear to think how it must have changed.'

He forced a smile as he embraced the three children. 'Hopefully, when you return you will see it in all its glory. Now go. Turn to the left as you leave the valley. Take the path through the woods and when you reach the river, turn left again and follow it upstream. There are many waterfalls tumbling down the steepest parts of the mountain, but surely, long before you reach the source, you will find running water.'

'Then what?' asked Merryn.

'We must trust The Gift to show you, for I cannot tell you more.'

Overcome with dismay, Merryn and Jake looked at one another.

Hamish, on the other hand, was quick to respond. 'Is that all?' he demanded. 'No advice, no instructions, no clues, nothing to help us?'

'Alas, no,' said The Great Wizard, 'and now I must rest. The battle exhausted me, my heart is aching for my son and I feel The Stone Spell beginning to slow my senses.'

He turned, walked unsteadily towards The Lodge and went inside.

Jake shrugged. 'Well, he wasn't much help. I hope he's right about water breaking the spell.'

'So do I,' said Hamish. 'If he's wrong we're stumped.'

As it wound its way between towering cliffs the valley did indeed become narrower. They followed its twists and turns until Hamish, who was hurrying ahead, called out that he'd reached the end. They stepped out into an open space and stood side by side, looking at the city that lay at the far side of a vast plain.

The Great Wizard had described it as the most beautiful of cities. It was hard to believe. The only beauty lay in the shapes of towers, domes and minarets, but there was neither life nor colour in them. They were like grey cardboard silhouettes against a dull grey sky.

'Somewhere among those buildings,' said Merryn, 'is Kester—Kester turned to stone.' As she spoke his name an overwhelming sadness washed over her and silent tears began to stream down her cheeks.

Hamish grasped her hand and his voice filled with excitement. 'The bottle,' he said, 'the bottle from The Urisk. I bet it's for tears. Give it to me and let me catch them.'

Merryn sniffed and fumbled in her pocket. Out came the ruby-red bottle with its decoration of green leaves and blue forget-me-not flowers. Hamish flipped the golden lid and placed the open bottle against one cheek after the other. He went on catching her tears until they finally stopped flowing. Then he closed the lid and handed the bottle back to her.

'Come on,' said Jake. 'The path goes into the wood. It looks dark and gloomy, but we'll have to take it.'

Merryn and Hamish followed him into the trees. All along the edge of the path were grasses, and above their heads huge branches rose to the sky. But even here, everything was made of stone. Beneath their feet the snap of stone twigs made the only sound in an otherwise silent world.

As their eyes adjusted to the dim light they began to notice other things. Stone bodies of bees and butterflies rested on the heads of stone flowers. Stone birds perched on stone bushes, and between the stone leaves they caught glimpses of stone deer, their stone ears pricked up as if they were listening for approaching danger.

'It's worse than Tobias thought,' said Merryn. 'People can't have touched all these things. The infection must spread in other ways too.'

Jake agreed. 'It may be in the water. What if…what if it's travelled all the way up the river…what then?'

'Don't think about it,' said Hamish. 'That would be too awful. Let's get a move on. We won't know until we get there.'

They hurried on until the light began to fade and they could no longer see the way ahead.

'We'll have to stop,' said Merryn. 'We can't risk missing the path in the dark. Let's try to get some sleep.'

With everything turned to stone there was no chance of a comfortable bed. The path that had been smoothed by the passage of feet was the best place they could find. They kicked the scatter of stone twigs aside, lay down on the rock-hard ground and slept.

When morning came, Merryn was first to open her eyes. She stood up, stretched her aching limbs and nudged the boys. 'Wake up,' she said. 'We must get on.'

She looked at her watch and saw that it had stopped at the time they left Kerrera with The Great Wizard. 'We're outside earth time,' she said. 'We'll have to be careful. One day has gone already. That means there are only six days left. We mustn't lose count.'

'And we have to walk back,' said Jake. 'We've used one day to get this far, so we need one day to get back from here.'

'So we've only got five days,' said Hamish. 'We'll have to turn back in two and a half, otherwise we'll be too late.' He jumped to his feet and set off along the track. 'Come on. Let's get a move on.'

It was impossible to gauge the passage of time. No sun shone in the sky, no hunger pangs came to tell them that it was lunchtime. They walked for a while and eventually came out of the wood into a field. Meandering through it was what had once been a river, but no water flowed. They stood on the bank and Merryn took out the bottle so that Hamish could catch the tears that she couldn't hold back.

'It's like concrete!' Jake exclaimed. 'When one of those big concrete mixers tips its load, it looks just like this.'

Hamish looked upstream. As far as he could see, there was no change in the surface of the river. 'Bother,' he said. 'It looks as if the spell can flow uphill. We'll just have to hope it hasn't gone far.'

His hope was in vain. As they walked on, there was nothing to see but stone. Gradually, the river narrowed, boulders poked through its grey stone surface, and on one of them, a stone otter stood with a stone fish clenched in its stone teeth. High above them, a tall mountain poked into the cold grey sky. They walked on and up, and they came to the first of the waterfalls that The Great Wizard had mentioned. Only it wasn't a waterfall at all. There was no sign of movement. There was no sound of rushing water.

'It's like waterfalls in a cold winter,' said Hamish. 'Remember when we had hard frosts and the waterfalls were made of ice.'

'But they were beautiful,' said Merryn. 'They were clean and white and sparkling, and we knew they were going to flow again because they dripped when the sun came out. These are dead and dreary and we don't know if they'll ever...'

She choked on a sob, and for the third time she collected her tears. She returned the bottle to her pocket and looked up towards the next stone waterfall. It seemed a long way ahead, but they trudged on and reached it just as darkness was closing in. Glad to take a rest after the long, hard climb, they lay down on a ledge underneath an overhanging rock.

'That's another day gone,' said Jake.

'And another day for the journey back,' said Hamish. 'We've only got a day and a half left. If we don't find water tomorrow, we're...'

'Don't you dare say we're stumped,' Merryn snapped. 'Just lie down, wish on your crystal and get some sleep.'

She lay awake for a long time, holding her amethyst pendulum and longing to hear the voices of Kester and Tobias. But her two dear friends were made of stone and she knew that stone could not speak. So she wished they would find water on the morrow. Then she frowned, because even if they found it, how could they take it back to the people who needed it? They had nothing to put it in. How could they have been so stupid? She felt the prick of tears behind her eyes and knew that she was about to weep. She put her hand in her pocket, pulled out the glass bottle and, once again, she caught her tears as they fell.

Chapter 34

Hamish woke first. He stretched and called out to Merryn and Jake. 'Come on, lazy bones. We've got to find water today.'

Jake leapt to his feet and the two boys set off up the mountain. Merryn followed up the side of one stone waterfall after another. All day they climbed. The stone river became narrower. The mountain grew steeper and after a particularly difficult climb they found their way blocked by a sheer cliff.

'This is it,' said Jake. 'There's nowhere else to go.'

'Yes there is,' said Hamish. 'Look. There's a ledge across the rock face and there's a cave behind it. I bet that's where the river starts.'

Merryn shuddered. 'It's getting dark,' she said, 'and there's nowhere to lie down. We'll have to sleep in the cave and that means walking across the ledge. It looks awfully narrow. I wish it was wider.'

'I wish there wasn't such a long drop,' said Jake. 'We'd be in a right mess if we fell off.'

Merryn tried not to think of falling. She put one hand on the rock and edged her way towards the cave. Half way along she caught a glimpse of all that lay below. She gasped, closed her eyes for a count of three, took a deep breath and went on. She reached the place where water used to flow over the ledge. Now it hung like a curtain of stone, but she'd reached the cave.

'I've made it,' she called as she ducked under an overhang. 'Come on, and whatever you do, don't look down.'

She crossed her fingers as she waited for Hamish and Jake to join her. When they were safely inside she relaxed a little and looked round. Where the river had once flowed there were threads of stone running across the rocky floor. She took out her crystal so that it illuminated the darkest recess of the cave. There she saw the source of the river. Thin rivulets of stone poured from a cleft in the wall, but there was neither sight nor sound of water.

She suspended her amethyst pendulum above the crevice. Nothing happened. Hamish and Jake joined her and they tried all three crystals together. Still nothing happened.

'We need to think about this,' said Jake. 'Perhaps one of the other Tokens will work. Let's try them all.'

'I don't think we should try anything tonight,' said Hamish. 'If we break the spell the water might come out in a rush. We'll have to get back along the ledge before it sweeps us away.'

'That's a good point,' said Merryn. 'I wouldn't dare cross in the dark. Let's get some sleep and try as soon as it's light.'

So they settled down for a third uncomfortable night on a bed of cold, hard stone.

As day dawned, Merryn looked out on a dull, grey world. The sky, like a flat grey canvas stretched away into the distance, but worse than the lack of colour was the absence of sound.

'Silent and still,' she murmured. 'It's as if we're the only people in the world.'

'I know,' said Hamish as he came to stand beside her. 'But today we'll find out if we can break the spell. If we manage it, there'll be wizards all over the place.'

Jake stood up and yawned. 'Then we'll be able to go home,' he said. 'I can't wait to see Rex. I'm missing him like mad and I can't believe he isn't missing me.'

Merryn emptied her pockets and spread the Tokens out on a flat rock. There was The Flint Arrowhead, the ruby-red bottle of tears and the silken bag containing the heart-stone.

'Let's add our hag-stones too,' she said.

Hamish put The Silver Chanter next to his hag-stone. Jake brought out the single pearl in its sequined purse. He added his hag-stone and re-arranged the items into a circle. He moved The Flint Arrowhead to the centre and as soon as he let go it began to spin. Flint to gold, gold to orange, orange to yellow, yellow to white and back again before it slowed and stopped.

'I didn't expect that', Merryn exclaimed as it pointed to the purse containing Sula's pearl.

'But if you think about it,' said Hamish,' it makes sense. Pearls are made in the sea so they have something to do with water.'

Jake nodded in agreement. He carried the pearl over to the crevice and pushed it inside. It fell from his hand and disappeared with a slight tinkle, but no water flowed.

'I've lost it,' he said, 'and it hasn't done anything. What a waste.'

'No,' said Merryn. 'Look, The Flint Arrowhead's spinning again. It's such a strong spell that it may need more than one Token to break it.'

Flint to gold, gold to orange, orange to yellow, yellow to white and back again. When it stopped it was pointing to The Silver Chanter.

Hamish, grinning all over his face, grabbed it. 'I told you there'd be a use for it. I've been looking after it so I'm going to blow it.'

He marched over to the crevice, lifted The Silver Chanter to his lips, puffed out his cheeks and gave a single blow. The sound that came out was unlike the chanters that he'd heard at school. It didn't seem to matter where he put his fingers. The music played itself. It rippled, gurgled and splashed like a small stream tumbling over rocks.

'It's enchanted water music,' said Merryn. 'Surely it's going to work.'

But the music stopped, and no matter how hard Hamish blew, it would not play again. Still the water refused to flow.

'Look,' Jake called, 'it's spinning again.'

Flint to gold, gold to orange, orange to yellow, yellow to white and back again. It slowed and wavered, as if it couldn't decide where to stop. Merryn chewed on her fingers. Jake clutched his crystal and willed The Flint Arrowhead to make a choice.

Hamish called out impatiently, 'Come on, what are you waiting for?'

The Flint Arrowhead would not be hurried. For several seconds it paused at the ruby-red bottle, but it continued to quiver before spinning again. Flint to gold, gold to orange, orange to yellow, yellow to white and back again. When it finally stopped it was pointing to the silken bag that contained the heart-stone.

Merryn gasped. 'It can't stop there. We have to save the heart-stone for our moment of greatest need.'

'Well this must be it,' said Jake. 'We've tried everything else and nothing works. It wants us to use the heart-stone so that's what we have to do.'

Merryn shook her head. 'No. We can't. I want it to be sure.'

She picked up the arrowhead and turned it to the ruby-red bottle. It swung back to the silken bag that held the heart-stone.

'It's made its mind up,' said Hamish. 'We've got to trust it. It's our last chance. If it doesn't work we'll still have time to get back to The Lodge.'

'Yes,' said Jake, 'and we can go home knowing we tried our best.'

'But our best might not be good enough,' Merryn wailed. 'I can't go home. I can't leave Kester turned to stone. I refuse to leave The Land of Benevolent Wizardry like this.' She stomped over to the cave entrance and looked out over the grey waste. 'It's dead and dismal and I can't bear it.' Hot angry tears ran down her cheeks.

'It's no good having a tantrum,' said Hamish, 'and don't waste those tears.' He grabbed the ruby-red bottle and went to catch them. 'Keep still, we might need them.'

Merryn tried to stop crying, but she couldn't stop the tears falling. 'Maybe you're right,' she sniffed. 'I'm sorry. If you both want me to use the heart-stone I will, but it isn't buzzing so I don't think it's ready.'

When all her tears were safely stored in the bottle, she dried her eyes and picked up the silken bag. She tipped the heart-stone into her palm and closed her fingers over it.

'Nothing's happening,' she said. 'I told you, it isn't ready.'

'Maybe you're not ready,' said Jake. 'The Fairy Woman said it would only work if you truly believed it. You don't think it's going to work so it won't. You'd better let me try.'

'And we'd better be ready to leave if it works,' said Hamish, 'or else we'll get washed away.'

Jake held out his hand and Merryn, with great reluctance, placed the heart-stone in his palm. He folded his other hand over it and closed his eyes. For a whole minute nothing happened, then his head began to nod rhythmically as if in time to a pulse that only he could feel.

Hamish nudged Merryn and raised both his thumbs. Jake turned towards the cleft at the back of the cave. He raised his arm to throw the heart-stone, but before he could do so, it rose of its own accord and flew to the source of the river.

Chapter 35

The heart-stone disappeared into the cleft at the back of the cave, but no sound of running water broke the silence. Merryn, who had expected nothing, turned away with an aching heart. Hamish brushed away tears of frustration and stuffed The Silver Chanter into his pocket along with his hag-stone.

Jake groaned with disappointment as he picked up his hag-stone. 'It should have worked.' He glared at Merryn. 'It's your fault because you didn't believe.'

Merryn winced at his angry words. She closed her eyes. Her thoughts raced back to Fang an t-Sithein and The Fairy Woman's voice came to her.

'Merryn, where is your faith? The heart-stone will not fail if you believe in its power.'

A picture of her last encounter with the heart-stone flitted through her mind. She recalled how it had responded to the witch's curse. How it had buzzed like a swarm of angry bees, circled the witch's head and destroyed her. Suddenly her mind cleared. If it could destroy that terrible witch, it could do anything. Her heart leapt and her faith returned.

At the same moment, Hamish shook her by the shoulder. 'Listen,' he said. 'I think it's starting to work.'

From deep within the cleft came a trickling sound and suddenly there was water. It gurgled and splashed as it ran down the rock and across the floor. Within seconds, it was pouring from the cave entrance, turning the curtain of stone into a rush of clear water.

'Quick,' said Hamish. 'We've got to get out.'

They grabbed the rest of the Tokens, and one behind the other, they stepped onto the ledge and edged their way to safety. The waterfall trebled in size. It was as if a huge underground lake had been held back and now it was rushing to escape.

They clambered down the side of the waterfall, and as rock and boulder grew damp with spray, grey stone turned to green of moss and fern. The pool at the base of the waterfall grew deeper. A dipper flew from behind the falling water, launched itself into the pool and emerged with a caddisfly larva in its beak. It landed on a boulder and stood, bobbing and curtseying in the middle of the growing river.

On ran the water, down a second waterfall and into another pool. The children hurried, trying to keep up with the flow, but it was all happening so quickly that they were soon left far behind. Ahead of them, the scene was changing. The river was a torrent of white water. From its banks, a film of green spread out across the land. Flowers burst into bloom, dragonflies hovered, bees buzzed and a glorious yellow butterfly landed at their feet.

'It's like spring and summer squashed into one day,' said Merryn.

'It's like those magic painting books, where you don't need paint,' said Jake. 'You just use water and the colours appear all by themselves.'

'It's like nothing on earth,' said Hamish. 'It's magic, wonderful, wonderful magic and we made it.'

He scrambled down a huge boulder and clattered down a heap of loose scree. An otter shot out from under his feet, bounded over the rocks and dived into the water. The river grew wider. The downward climb grew easier, far easier than the upward struggle of the previous days. They passed the place where they'd slept two nights ago and there was still plenty of daylight in the sky. By the time darkness fell they lay down on a soft grassy bed, and when they looked up, the dull grey sky had been replaced by millions of twinkling stars.

Merryn wasn't sure why she woke early. Was it the first rays of sun warming her face? Or was it bird song —skylarks singing in the blue above, or a tiny wren trilling from a nearby bush? She sat up and saw that the boys were still asleep. Not far away she could see the trees of the woodland. They were as green as the grass that she lay on. The river was still flowing, meandering in great curves towards the city and the hills beyond. The mountain rose behind her, its expanse of stone broken by the river that they'd released from The Stone Spell.

She jumped to her feet. 'Come on, wake up,' she cried. 'I think we can reach The Lodge before nightfall. It's downhill all the way and I can already see the wood.'

Hamish yawned. 'The seven days aren't up until the day after tomorrow. What's the hurry?'

'That doesn't sound right,' said Jake, 'I think tomorrow's our last day. I've lost count but I don't care. The sooner we get to The Lodge the sooner we can go home.'

Merryn sighed as they set out to follow the river. 'That's all very well,' she said. 'We've broken the spell and things are coming back to life. You can go home if you want, but I'm not going anywhere until I've seen Kester. I'd like to see the city too. '

'So would I,' said Hamish. 'We're the first mortals to visit and I expect we'll be the last. I think we deserve a holiday.'

Jake frowned. 'Are you absolutely sure Rex isn't missing me?'

'Positive,' said Merryn. 'It's happened to us loads of times. Our parents never miss us. We're in a different time zone. When we get back it'll still be Sunday and we'll still be on the hilltop with Rex.'

'OK, if you're absolutely sure,' said Jake. 'I don't suppose we'll ever get this chance again. An extra day or two might be fun.'

On their way to the mountain they'd been so overawed by the sight of the stone river that they hadn't looked at anything else. They'd concentrated on heading upwards, aware that everything around them had been turned to stone. Now, as they reached the level plain, the land was filled with colour. Ahead of them, a field of blue-green wheat was bright with scarlet poppies. Beyond that, a herd of brown cows grazed on a lush, flower-filled pasture. Soon they reached the place where the path turned towards the wood. Merryn stopped, looked both ways and hesitated.

'Look,' she said as she pointed to a clump of trees farther down the river. 'I can see the roof of a cottage. There must be people there. I want to check that they're all right. Let's go there first. It won't take long.'

They hurried on, only hesitating when a black and white collie came out of its kennel to bark a warning. Although the outside of the cottage was wreathed in climbing roses, the blue-painted door was closed. The dog barked again, but the door didn't open. Yet there were signs of life everywhere. Speckled hens and a handsome cockerel pecked at fallen grain. Half a dozen white ducks splashed in a circular pond and fan-tailed doves cooed from the roof of an old-fashioned well. A carthorse drank from a stone trough. Water dripped from its mouth as it raised its head to gaze at them with soft brown eyes. Merryn tapped cautiously on the cottage door, and a ginger cat with three assorted kittens ran from the barn, mewed loudly and rubbed against her legs.

'Here,' said Jake as he pushed in front of her. 'Let me try.' He hammered on the door, waited a moment and hammered again.

'It's no good,' said Hamish. 'We'll have to go in. It looks as if the heart-stone's magic stopped at the door.'

Without waiting for a response he tried to push the door. It wouldn't move. It took all three of them to open it wide enough to slip inside.

'Just as I thought,' he said,' everything's stone. Look, even the inside of the door is stone. That's why it was hard to get in. How odd is that when the outside's changed back to wood?'

They tip-toed round the house, searching the kitchen with its stone pots and pans. They looked into a larger room with stone armchairs, a stone rocking chair and a stone fire in a stone fireplace. They climbed the stone stairs and looked through the half-open doors. There they found the people of the house. There was an old lady in one room, and a bearded man and his wife huddled together in another. In the third room, two children lay in stone bunks and a baby slept in a stone cradle. All six of them lay under stone bedclothes with their stone heads resting on stone pillows.

'Water,' said Jake. 'We must get water.' He dashed downstairs and out into the farmyard. The dog's dish, lying by the kennel was the only container he could see. He rinsed it in the trough, filled it with water and was about to carry it into the house when Merryn stopped him.

'It's dirty,' she said. 'The animals drink from the trough. We can't use that.'

She crossed to the well. 'It's like the one in my Nursery Rhyme book,' she said. 'You turn the handle and it lowers a bucket. Look, like this.'

When the bucket was filled, Hamish wound it up and unhooked it. They carried it upstairs and sprinkled water on the farmer's face. They tried to force drops through his stone lips, but it was useless. The farmer did not come back to life.

Chapter 36

Merryn turned away from the stone figures and ran downstairs. 'I can't bear it, and I can't understand why it isn't working.'

She threw herself into the stone rocking chair and closed her eyes. A few minutes later she realised that the chair was no longer made of stone. She ran her hands down the smooth wooden arms and felt the softness of the cushion under her bottom. She opened her eyes and looked round the room. The magic had crept in through the open door and the room had changed. She crossed to the window, opened the curtain and let the sun shine in.

'Jake, Hamish,' she cried, 'come down. I think it's going to be all right.'

There was a clatter on the stone stairs, but before the boys were halfway down, the clattering changed to creaking as stone turned to wood beneath their feet.

'Wow!' said Hamish as he dashed into the room.

He looked back the way he'd come. 'It's going upstairs,' he said, 'so it's just a matter of time before it reaches the people.' He ran back and watched as the last stone step changed to wood.

'Open all the curtains,' said Jake, 'the sun might speed it up.' He ran into the kitchen, threw back the curtains and opened the back door.

Hamish couldn't open the bedroom curtains because they were still made of stone. He looked down. 'It's moving along the floor,' he called. 'Come and see.'

Jake and Merryn ran to join him. They watched the slow creep of colour across the wooden floorboards, over striped rugs, a pair of pink slippers, and up the flower-patterned curtains and the legs of the bed.

'We shouldn't watch,' said Merryn. 'When they wake up and see us they'll think... ' She shook her head. 'I don't know what they'll think, but they might be scared. Come on, we'll wait outside. When we hear them moving about we'll knock on the door and wait for an answer.'

They went out into the sunshine, happy to see the beauty around them, but listening anxiously for the family to come to life. Time passed. Although the hens clucked contentedly, the doves cooed and the kittens purred there were no sounds from inside the cottage.

'I can't wait another minute,' said Hamish. 'It's been ages. It must have reached them by now. Perhaps they're just sleeping. I'm going to wake them up.'

'Don't,' said Merryn. 'Wait a bit longer.'

'We can't. We've got to get back to The Lodge,' said Jake. Ignoring Merryn's instruction he knocked on the door. It was no use. There was no reply.

Hamish stuck his head through the doorway and shouted. 'Hello, is anyone about?'

He went to the bottom of the stairs and called again. No one appeared. He and Jake tip-toed upstairs and peered into the main bedroom. The brass bedstead shone in the bright sunlight. The floral patterned quilt looked soft and inviting. Everything had changed except the farmer and his wife. Although their heads now lay on soft white pillows they were still made of stone.

Jake checked the old woman, the children and the baby. It was the same story. They were still locked in The Stone Spell. Unable to find an explanation they went downstairs in silence.

Merryn was pacing up and down in front of the open door. 'Well,' she demanded. 'What happened? What did you find? Did our spell reach the bedrooms?'

'It did,' said Jake. 'The beds have changed, but the people haven't.'

'The heart-stone wasn't strong enough,' said Hamish. 'What do we do now?'

'I can't believe it,' said Merryn. 'I won't believe it. We've missed something or we've done something wrong.'

She pulled The Flint Arrowhead from her pocket and placed it on the doorstep. It began to spin, flint to gold, gold to orange, orange to yellow, yellow to white and back again. When it stopped it was pointing to the gate through which they'd come.'

'That means we've to go back,' said Jake.

'Not all the way to the cave,' Hamish groaned. 'There isn't time.'

'If that's what it's telling us to do, we'll have to do it,' said Merryn, 'but I don't think it is. It isn't pointing to the mountain.'

'So where is it pointing?' Hamish ran to the gate and looked straight ahead. He turned back and grinned. 'The river, it's pointing to the river.'

'We used the wrong water,' said Jake. 'The heart-stone's spell isn't in the well. It's in the river. We've got to use river water. Come on, what are you waiting for?'

He started to run and then turned back with a sheepish grin. 'I'd better get something to put it in.'

In a matter of minutes the boys were running across the pasture with a couple of clanking buckets. Merryn followed with a huge jug clutched in her arms. At the river they stood on stepping-stones, filled their containers and set off back to the farm. The return journey was hard, no matter how careful the boys were, the water slopped out of the buckets and by the time they climbed the stairs, a third of it was lost.

'Let's try the farmer first,' said Hamish.

'No,' said Jake, 'Try his wife.'

'Try them both together,' said Merryn. 'They'll be so happy to see one another they won't notice us.'

They sprinkled river water on the stone faces. They dripped drops onto the stone lips and they stood back, watching and waiting. There was a slight movement of the woman's head and the man's hand stretched out from under the bedclothes.

Merryn grabbed the boys and pulled them onto the landing.

'You treat the children,' she said, 'and I'll see to the old woman. As soon as they start to stir, come back downstairs. We mustn't frighten them.'

A few minutes later, they stood in the yard listening for sounds from inside the cottage. The silence ended as heavy footsteps crossed the bedroom floor and thudded down the stairs. They were just about to knock when the door opened, and out came the farmer. He stared at them in surprise and demanded to know who they were and what they wanted.

'We're friends of The Great Wizard,' said Merryn. 'He sent us to break The Stone Spell.'

The farmer's jaw dropped. He looked stunned before turning back the way he'd come. 'Tabitha,' he cried as he ran back into the cottage. 'Tabitha, we're saved.'

Voices rose and fell. The farmer re-appeared with his wife. A baby lay in her arms, and a boy and a girl, still in their nightclothes, clung to her skirt. Close behind came the old woman with pink slippers on her feet.

Slowly they stepped out into the sunshine. The dog ran to them, wagging its tail, the horse whinnied and the children bent to pet the cat and her kittens. The old woman reached up, plucked a rose, held it to her cheek and began to weep.

The farmer's wife was the first to find her voice. 'We thought the end had come,' she said. 'How can we ever thank you?'

'There's no need,' said Merryn, 'seeing you all looking well and happy is thanks enough.'

The farmer grasped each of their hands in turn. 'I know of you,' he said. 'Tobias Witchbane said our only hope lay in two children—possessors of The Gift from the land that is called Earth. But there are three of you. How can that be? '

Hamish shrugged and pointed at Merryn. 'I haven't got The Gift but she's my sister and I always go with her.' Blushing with embarrassment he looked down at his feet. 'I sort of…came along for the ride.'

'Now that you are safe, we will leave you,' said Merryn. 'We must take our news back to The Great Wizard.'

'May all that is good preserve you,' said Tabitha. 'But, is there anything we can do to help?'

'Yes,' said Jake. 'We broke The Stone Spell at the source of the river and it seems to have cured the land, but it couldn't get inside your cottage. We had to force the door to let it in.'

'Even then,' said Merryn, 'we needed river water to bring you back to life. So please go, visit your neighbours, open their doors, wet their lips with water from the river, scatter it on their faces and tell them to do the same for others. Do that and your lives and your land will soon be back to normal.'

Chapter 37

'We will do all we can,' said the farmer. 'I will go to the nearest village without delay.'

'And we will be on our way,' said Merryn. 'The Great Wizard will be worrying and we must let him know that The Stone Spell is broken. We wanted to reach The Lodge before nightfall but I don't think we'll manage it now.'

'We could if you gave us a lift,' said Hamish. 'It's a long way and we've been walking for days.'

'Of course,' said the farmer. 'Children, get dressed while I harness Beauty to the cart.' He turned back to Hamish. 'We can take you through the wood, but we must leave you at the end of the track. The valley is only for those who are leaving our land, or returning to it. I understand it is a no-man's land, a place between worlds where different rules apply.

'We must take river water,' said Merryn, 'but we need something to put it in.'

'I'll get a milk churn,' said the farmer.

'I'll fetch bottles,' said Tabitha as she went back indoors.

The farmer harnessed Beauty, the children climbed into the cart and they headed for the river. They used ladles to fill the churn and when six bottles had been filled they turned towards the track through the wood. Merryn gave a smile of contentment when she saw the beauty of the woodland. Trees were not only clothed in green, but were covered with fragrant blossom. Brightly coloured flowers grew along the track edge and the air was alive with speckled butterflies and tiny parachutes of dandelion seeds. Beauty trotted along at a spanking pace. They passed the place where they'd slept on the first night of their adventure and soon they reached the entrance to the valley.

The farmer stepped down and manhandled the churn to the side of the track. He turned Beauty in a wide curve. Then, with a cheery wave and many words of thanks he headed back to the farm.

'Look across the plain,' said Merryn. 'The city is free of The Stone Spell.'

They gazed at the breathtaking sight of glittering spires, towers, domes and minarets in colours that they'd never seen before. The Stone Spell was broken and the worst part of their adventure was over, but when they turned into the valley their high spirits disappeared. Everything was as grey and gloomy as ever.

'It hasn't broken here,' said Jake. 'Something's stopped it from getting into the valley.'

'But what could do that?' asked Hamish. 'It's not like the cottage. There isn't a door to keep it out.'

'The farmer said there are different rules here,' said Merryn. 'Maybe it's always like this,'

'I don't think so,' said Jake. 'There's something wrong and I don't like it.'

'There's only one way to find out,' said Hamish. 'Let's go to The Lodge and then we'll know.'

They followed the twists and turns of the narrow valley until The Lodge came into view. They broke into a run and by the time they reached the open door they had to pause to catch their breath.

'Nothing's changed,' said Hamish, 'and where's The Great Wizard?'

'I'm here.' A voice from the far end of the room was barely a whisper.

They dashed across to find him slumped in a corner, his head thrown back, his mouth open, his eyes closed.

Merryn fell to her knees. She splashed his face with river water and held the bottle to his lips, but it was no use. As soon as the water touched him, it turned to stone.

'Water,' he gasped. 'You found water, but it is too late for me.'

'It works for people who have already turned to stone,' said Merryn. 'We'll cure Tobias. He'll know what to do.'

But Hamish and Jake had already tried to wake Tobias. They had wet his face and forced water between his stone lips, but he had not responded. Of his grandson there was no sign, but there were stone doors that refused to open and they guessed that he must lie behind one of them

Merryn took The Great Wizard's hands in her own and looked into his eyes.

'We reached the source of the river and we made the water flow. The land is green again. The Stone Spell is breaking but it can't get past closed doors and it hasn't spread into this valley. We found a farm and we gave river water to the family. They are alive and carrying water to the next village. They will open doors and send people out to help their neighbours, so the cure will spread.'

The Great Wizard sighed. 'It is good, but it is only half a cure. What does Tobias suggest?'

'He won't wake,' said Hamish. 'We've tried.'

'The heart-stone's magic has to come into the valley,' Jake explained. 'It has to come into The Lodge and change everything back from stone. When that happens we think we can wake Tobias.'

'At least that's how it worked at the farm,' said Hamish.

'But why won't it come into the valley?' Merryn asked.

'There must be some vestige of The Grand High Witch's magic,' said The Great Wizard. 'Her spells must be embedded in the rocks. I can think of no other reason.'

'So how do we get rid of them?' asked Hamish.

'With great difficulty, if at all,' said The Great Wizard. 'We need the combined power of all our wizards. You must go to the city to release them.'

'That means we'll have to stay a bit longer,' said Jake. 'If we can cure the other wizards they can come back and make everything right.'

'I thought you were keen to go home,' said Hamish.

'I was and I am,' said Jake,' but we can't leave things half finished. In any case, we'd better stick together and Merryn won't leave until she's seen Kester.'

'Ah! Kester,' said The Great Wizard. 'Find my son. Cure him and I will be in your debt forever. I wish I could come with you, but my strength fails me. Your news has given me hope, but I am too weak to travel. Go, make haste, free my wizards and send them to me.'

'There's no point in leaving any water,' said Merryn as she picked up her bottles, 'and we may need them along the way.'

'Not when you reach the city,' said The Great Wizard. 'The river runs through the middle of it, and if you are right, it will be flowing again.'

Hamish and Jake collected their bottles and headed out of the door.

Merryn paused. 'Wait. I want to check that we're doing the right thing.'

She took out The Flint Arrowhead and placed it on the doorstep. It began to spin—flint to gold, gold to orange, orange to yellow, yellow to white and back again. When it stopped it was pointing back the way they'd come, back down the valley in the direction of the city.

Once again they hurried along the twists and turns until they reached the open plain. The grey world was left behind and the city lay ahead. It was farther, much farther than they'd realised. They walked on, but it was still impossibly distant when the sun started to sink behind the hills.

'We're not going to make it before nightfall,' said Merryn. 'We'll have to find somewhere to sleep.'

'Not yet,' said Jake, 'let's keep going until it's too dark to see.'

As it turned out, there was no need to stop. A glorious sunset turned the sky to shades of pink and violet. When the colours faded, a full moon rising above the distant mountain lit their way, and as dawn was breaking they reached the silent city. Buildings rose, tall and elegant on either side of broad streets. The river ran under a series of bridges, and all along its banks were trees, flowerbeds and carved wooden benches.

Hamish grabbed Merryn by the arm and pointed. 'Look, I think I can see someone.'

Filled with hope they ran to one of the benches and there they found a wizard. His stone elbow rested on the wooden arm of the bench and his stone cheek was cupped in his stone hand. Unlike the others they'd seen, his stone eyes were open as if he was gazing at the sunlight dancing on the river.

Jake opened one of his bottles. He splashed river water over the stone face and dripped water on the stone lips. Merryn and Hamish held up the crossed fingers of both hands. Then they stood back, watching, waiting and wishing.

Chapter 38

The only movement was of water trickling down the wizard's stone beard. Hamish clutched Merryn's arm and Jake threw up his hands in defeat. But a moment later, the wizard yawned, blinked, stared at the river and blinked again. His face broke into a smile when he caught sight of Merryn.

'I know you,' he said, 'although a great deal has happened since you helped us to trap The Clickfinger Locket. I remember your face and your name, Merryn MacQueen. Yours too, Hamish, although I do not know how you come to be in The Land of Benevolent Wizardry.'

Hamish looked down at his shoes. 'I know I shouldn't be here, but I couldn't let Merryn go without me. I grabbed hold of her and we came with The Great Wizard.'

'It's a good thing he did,' said Merryn. 'We couldn't have managed without him.'

'Then he is welcome,' said the wizard, 'and this must be Jake, the boy with The Gift. I am glad to meet you. I see the river is flowing and I, Orlando, am awake, so you have broken The Stone Spell. I would love to know the secret of your success.'

'But it isn't a complete success,' said Merryn. 'The river flows again and we can use the water to bring people back to life, but you're the only one alive in the entire city.'

Orlando's expression changed to one of astonishment. 'But how can that be? And what of Tobias and The Great Wizard?'

'Infected,' said Jake. 'We must free all the wizards and send them to The Lodge of The Portal. The Grand High Witch followed us...'

Orlando gasped. 'Such a thing should not have been possible. Where is she now? How...?'

'Don't bother about her,' Hamish cut in. 'She'd dead and so is The Snake Wand.'

'But she left some magic behind,' said Merryn. 'Our spell is spreading but it can't get into the valley and it can't go through closed doors.

There was a look of bewilderment on Orlando's face. He stood shaking his head as he tried to make sense of what they were saying.

'Forget the details,' said Jake. 'Just show us where the wizards are. We'll release them, then they can go to The Lodge to free Tobias and his grandson.'

'And The Great Wizard,' said Hamish. 'He caught The Stone Spell, but he hasn't turned to stone yet. If we hurry we can save him too.'

Orlando leapt to his feet. 'First we must go to my house. My father and brothers are there. They are powerful wizards. Free them and they will help.'

He led them through deserted streets until he came to a house with a huge elaborately carved front door. 'This is it,' he said as he tried, unsuccessfully, to open it.

'Let me help.' Hamish put his shoulder against the door and pushed with all his might. Then he stepped back and shrugged. 'It must be locked.'

'Locked? We have no need of locks in our land,' said Orlando.

'It's still stone on the inside,' said Merryn. 'It's too heavy, that's all.'

228

She and Jake stepped forwards, and when the four of them pushed together, the door opened the merest crack. The magic seeped inside and soon they were able to follow.

Orlando bounded up the stone staircase and stopped on the landing. 'My father,' he said. 'Free my father first.'

'We can't,' said Merryn. 'The door is still made of stone. Now the front door is open, the spell will creep upstairs, but we'll have to wait until this side of the door has turned back to wood. It isn't a large door. Hamish should be able to open it by himself so he can stay here. He can wake your father and your brothers when the time is right.'

'But...' said Hamish.

'No arguments,' said Merryn. 'Jake and I will go with Orlando. Front doors are much heavier. It may take all three of us to open them.'

Leaving Hamish to watch the slow spread of magic, they hurried down highways and byways, forcing open doors as they went. Merryn, unable to hold back any longer, asked the question that was foremost in her mind.

'Where is Kester?'

'As The Great Wizard's son and heir, his home is with his father,' said Orlando. He pointed to a house on the opposite side of the river. 'That is where you will find him.'

'I must go,' said Merryn. 'You two can free the other wizards.'

'I will take them to The Lodge of The Portal,' said Orlando, 'and when you have released Kester you must join us. We will need all our combined power to remove the remnants of The Grand High Witch's magic.'

Leaving Jake and Orlando behind, Merryn ran along the embankment, crossed a bridge and made her way towards The Great Wizard's house. She passed through ornate gates and tried to push the heavy door open. It refused to move, so she splashed it with river water and suspended her amethyst pendulum above the door handle. At her third attempt she was able to squeeze inside. It was as she'd expected, everything was locked in stone, but the magic was already entering. Soon it was spreading up the stairs, passing along the landing and changing the doors to wood. She opened them all, and although there were stone people on each of the stone beds it wasn't until she came to the last room that she found Kester. He was not alone. A woman sat in a chair beside his bed. Her stone hand rested on his chest and a trail of stone tears lay on her cheek.

Merryn opened the bottle of river water, dampened Kester's face and held the bottle to his lips. Time seemed to stand still. She tried again, a second and a third time, but Kester did not stir. In desperation she splashed the woman's face and held river water to her lips. In a very short time the stone hands loosened their grip and the stone face glowed with life.

'Kester,' the woman cried. She leant over and kissed his stone forehead. 'Kester, my son, soon the children will arrive with The Gift, and then...'

'I'm already here,' said Merryn. 'I have The Gift and I've restored the land, but I cannot bring Kester back to life. I've tried three times and I've failed. I don't understand because I did exactly the same for you, and it worked.'

The woman took Merryn's hand. 'I am Kester's mother, Penelope, and you are Merryn MacQueen. You saved my son once and you must save him again.'

'But I told you,' said Merryn. 'I've tried and I can't do it.'

'Then try again,' Penelope ordered.

For the fourth time, Merryn dampened Kester's stone face and wetted his stone lips. Penelope gripped her hand as they waited to see what would happen. Minutes passed and there was no change, no sign of movement, nothing to indicate that The Stone Spell was breaking.

'I don't understand,' said Merryn. 'Perhaps the spell is stronger in him than in anyone else. Maybe The Grand High Witch added something just for him, something that needs an extra special cure.'

'Then save my husband's brothers,' said Penelope. 'They are all wizards and may be able to help. I will stay with Kester until you return.'

With great reluctance Merryn left Kester. She went into one room after another. There, without difficulty, she brought Kester's uncles back to life. Quickly, she explained the need for them to go to The Lodge of The Portal. 'But first,' she said, 'I need more river water to save everyone else in the house.'

The wizards were quick to respond. Most of them left for The Lodge while others returned with jugs of river water. Merryn brought one women back to life, and told her how to break the spell for everyone in the house—and for everyone throughout the city. Soon the air was filled with chatter and laughter. But Merryn didn't feel like chattering or laughing. Still puzzling over her failure to save Kester, she hurried back to his room.

'Why are you alone?' asked Penelope. 'Where are my husband's brothers?'

They've gone to The Lodge to help Tobias and The Great Wizard,' said Merryn. 'The Stone Spell still has a hold over the valley and all the wizards are needed to break it. Kester and I have to join them, but first I must bring him back to life. I have one last thing to try and I daren't think what will happen if it fails.'

She reached into her pocket and took out the ruby-red bottle with its pattern of green leaves and blue forget-me-not flowers. She flipped back the golden lid and wiped Kester's face with her tears. Slowly, very slowly he opened his eyes, sat up and grasped her hands.

'Merryn,' he said. 'I knew you would not fail me.'

Chapter 39

'Come,' said Kester. 'Now that you are here I will show you the beauty of our city.'

'That would be unwise,' said Penelope. 'Merryn is not of our people. You should not spend time together. You must not... You cannot...'

'I must and I can,' said Kester. 'She saved my life for the second time and I will spend time with her before she leaves.'

Despite Penelope's protests he led Merryn into the sunlit garden. 'First we will...'

Merryn put her finger to his lips. 'First we must go to The Lodge of the Portal because the valley is still locked in The Stone Spell.'

'But how can that be?'

'I do not know,' she said, 'but your father and Tobias are there and they need us.'

Kester gasped. 'Don't tell me that they too were infected.'

'Tobias was and your father has only a few days before he turns to stone.'

Her hand flew to her mouth and her eyes widened in fear. 'I've done the most stupid thing. I told the wizards to go to The Lodge. What if they turn back to stone and the spell starts to spread again?'

The change from Kester the young wizard to Kester the horse was instantaneous. Within seconds Merryn had mounted—and within minutes they were out of the city and heading across the plain. To her, riding through the countryside with Kester was the best thing in the world, but not this time. All she could think of was the horror that might lie ahead. But as they neared the end of their journey, relief flooded through her. The wizards were waiting at the valley entrance. They were standing in silence, but when they recognised Kester a great cheer rang out.

'Wait.' Merryn shouted. 'Don't go into the valley.'

Kester the horse changed back into Kester the wizard. 'Merryn saved me,' he cried, 'and now she will help us to break The Stone Spell.'

Orlando stepped forward with Jake and Hamish at his side. 'She told us to go to The Lodge,' he said, 'but when the first wizard stepped into the valley he was re-infected. He turned to stone in an instant.'

Merryn gasped. She stood breathing heavily, colour draining from her face. 'I'm sorry,' she said. 'I was wrong. Is he…?'

'Don't worry,' Jake cut in. 'We dragged him out and gave him river water and he's back to normal.' He grinned and gave a half-hearted laugh. 'If you can ever call a wizard normal.'

Kester grasped Merryn's arm. 'Do not blame yourself,' he said. 'It was a small mistake, but it is clear that the wizards cannot enter the valley. The solution is therefore up to you and Jake and The Gift.'

'And me,' said Hamish.'

'Hamish,' Kester exclaimed. 'I had not expected to see you here, but you have helped your sister in the past and I am sure that you can help her again.'

'I can,' said Hamish.' I may not have The Gift, but I know what to do next.' He turned to Merryn. 'Ask The Flint Arrowhead.'

The three children stepped towards the grey forbidding entrance to the valley. The green of the grassy plain, the brightly coloured flowers, the blue of the sky and the chirruping of birds all ended here. Beyond, was the power of The Grand High Witch. Even though she and The Snake Wand had been defeated it was obvious that a great deal of their evil magic remained.

The wizards watched as Merryn placed The Flint Arrowhead on the ground. Now the Tokens were few. The pearl had already served its purpose. It lay up the mountain in a crevice in a cave at the source of the river. The heart-stone, after making the water flow again, had returned to The Fairy Woman on Tiree. All that remained were The Silver Chanter, the Selkie's empty purse and the bottle that contained Merryn's last few tears. These were placed on either side of The Flint Arrowhead.

Merryn knew the answer before the arrowhead started to spin, but she watched and waited until she was sure she was right. The arrowhead spun—flint to gold, gold to orange, orange to yellow, yellow to white and back again.

'I knew it,' she said as the arrowhead pointed to the ruby-red bottle. 'I don't know why, but the answer is in my tears.'

She looked up at Kester. 'Four times I failed to save you with river water, but my tears brought you back to life. You're cured, and if I'm right, you can enter the valley without harm.'

Murmurs of disbelief and anxiety passed round the crowd of wizards.

'But what if you are wrong?' Orlando asked. 'It is a great risk.'

'It is a risk I must take,' said Kester. 'I must do all in my power to save my father and my uncle. Besides, I have faith in Merryn. I trust her with my life.'

He walked to the mouth of the valley and passed between the rocky walls. No one else moved. Every breath was held as wizards and mortals waited to see what would happen. A few moments later, Kester re-appeared and a second great cheer rang out across the plain.

'Come,' he said to Merryn, Jake and Hamish. 'We must not waste time. I will carry all three of you.'

In an instant he stood before them, a handsome young stallion, his flanks gleaming, his mane and tail lifting in the breeze. Merryn mounted, and with Jake and Hamish behind her they entered the valley.

Kester's hooves clip-clopped on the stone floor as they passed between high rocky walls. After the twists and turns of the track, the narrow passage widened and The Lodge of the Portal came into view. Kester cantered over the remaining distance and stopped outside the door. They slid from his back and he immediately returned to his wizard form.

'It is worse than I feared,' he said. 'I had no idea that the spell had affected everything. I thought it was just people and the things they touched. The valley was never like this.'

'Your whole country was like this,' said Merryn. 'The city, the mountains, even the river was turned to stone. We climbed to the source to break the spell. When the water flowed again our magic spread through the land, but something stopped it from getting into the valley.'

Kester didn't wait to hear more. He grabbed Merryn's hand. 'Come. Take me to my father.'

They stepped through the half-open door to find Tobias sitting exactly as they had left him. Kester passed a hand over his eyes and looked away.

'All of us?' he asked. 'Every single wizard looked like that?

'Everyone except your father,' said Merryn. 'He was infected on the day we arrived.'

'And he hasn't turned to stone yet,' said Hamish, 'but he looks awful.'

Kester hurried to where his father lay. He fell on his knees and touched The Great Wizard's cold face.

Merryn flipped the lid of the ruby-red bottle and dropped a few tears on The Great Wizard's lips. Almost at once, his eyes opened. He sat up and Merryn knew that she'd finally found the cure for The Stone Spell.

'My son,' The Great Wizard embraced Kester. 'You are safe.'

He grasped Merryn's hand. 'And we have you to thank.'

Merryn left father and son to rejoice in their recovery and she went to Tobias. She applied her tears to his lips and then she stood back to watch.

'It's working,' said Hamish as the pen slipped from the wizard's fingers. 'He's coming back to life even though everything else is made of stone.'

Tobias looked up at the three children. 'Merryn, Jake you are well come indeed—and Hamish too, how can this be?'

'It's a long story,' said Hamish.

'Soon you'll know it all,' said Merryn, 'but there's more work to do. We've cured the wizards, but the valley and The Lodge are still locked in stone.'

Tobias looked round. 'My grandson,' he asked, 'have you saved him too?'

Merryn shook her head. 'Not yet, show me where he is and it will only take a moment.'

Tobias crossed the stone room and grasped the stone handle on one of the stone doors. He tried to turn it, but it wouldn't move. 'He is in there. When he turned to stone I could not bear to look at him. I closed the door and left him. But what do we do now? If we cannot open the door, if we cannot break the rest of The Stone Spell he will remain as stone for ever.'

Chapter 40

Merryn wept at the thought of the stone child locked in a stone room behind a stone door that wouldn't open. She ran out of The Lodge and sat down on the stone doorstep. Tears coursed down her cheeks and she knew she must catch them. As they dripped into the ruby-red bottle she heard voices drifting from The Lodge.

The Great Wizard was speaking. His voice was grave. 'The valley is locked in The Stone Spell because malevolent magic still remains. The other wizards cannot set foot in the valley so they cannot help us to dispel it. It is up to us, three mortals and three wizards against whatever The Grand High Witch and The Snake Wand left behind.'

'I hate to mention this,' said Tobias,' but it is not only our future that is at stake. As long as The Portal is locked in stone we cannot leave our land to take these brave children home.'

There was a long silence while they tried to find a solution to their shared problem. The Great Wizard stepped outside, leaned against the wall and closed his eyes. Tobias paced backwards and forwards in front of The Lodge. Kester and Jake sat down next to Merryn. Hamish went over to the desk and absentmindedly picked up the pen that Tobias had been using. His fingers closed on something that definitely wasn't made of stone. He blinked, looked at the Log Book, blinked and looked again. That too had changed.

He watched until he was certain that his eyes weren't deceiving him. Merryn's tears had woken

Tobias and the magic had spread from him to the pen. From the pen it had passed to the Log Book. Tentatively he turned a page, just to make sure. Now, very slowly, the spell was breaking. Grey stone was turning to polished wood as the cure moved across the desk. When it crept down the desk legs and started to cross the floor he could no longer contain his excitement.

'It's over,' he shouted. 'The Stone Spell is breaking. Come and see.'

Jake, Merryn and Kester were the first to run inside. The Great Wizard and Tobias came next. They all watched as the magic crept up the walls and turned the windows to glass. Tobias ran to the door that had refused to open earlier. He turned the handle and flung it open. Merryn, chasing after him, found him on his knees next to his grandson. Quickly she opened the ruby-red bottle and wetted the boy's stone lips.

'Grandpa,' said the child as he opened his eyes. 'I knew you'd make me better.'

'Not I,' said Tobias. 'Merryn is the one we have to thank.'

The Great Wizard turned to Merryn. 'Your tears came from your heart. They were pure and honest and good. The evil of The Grand High Witch had no defence against them. It was not just the river water. It was not even The Gift that banished the last remnants of her spell. It was the love and concern that flowed through your tears.'

'Wow,' said Hamish, 'and I always thought it was babyish to cry.'

'Not so,' said Tobias. 'It is good to cry if the reason behind the tears is an honest one.'

By the time they stepped out of The Lodge, the magic had crept into the valley and was making its way along the track. The plants that grew on the cliffs turned to shades of green. Flowers burst into bloom. The grey sky brightened to blue. A ray of sun illuminated the grass and a bird began to sing. Their faces broke into smiles. They hugged one another and laughed with joy as they followed the spread of magic down the valley. Long before they reached the plain, they knew that it had gone before them, for suddenly there were sounds of great excitement.

Orlando and his brothers were coming to meet them. Merryn, Jake and Hamish were lifted into the air and carried on the wizards' shoulders. When they emerged from the mouth of the valley, the cheer that greeted them was loud enough to travel far across the land.

As if from nowhere, people came, lining the track, waving and cheering. Crowds followed them across the plain and when they reached the city, it was bright with coloured flags and the sounds of triumphant music. There was dancing in the streets and as night began to fall, thousands of lanterns shone out into the darkness. Every tree and every bridge was festooned with lights and the river rippled with reflections in colours that were beyond the colours of rainbows.

All night long the celebrations continued, but when dawn began to break, The Great Wizard called for silence. The people paused in their dancing. The music stopped. The sound of happy voices died away.

When all was quiet, The Great Wizard began to speak. 'We are forever indebted to our three young friends. They braved great dangers to come to our aid, but now I must keep my promise. Bid them farewell, for Kester, Tobias and I must take them back to Earth.'

As they passed through the crowds, it seemed that everyone wanted to touch them. They were hugged and kissed, their hands were shaken, their backs were patted and their ears were filled with words of gratitude. Jake grinned from ear to ear, delighted to be going home to Rex. He wasn't at all sorry to leave The Land of Benevolent Wizardry. Hamish puzzled over a mixture of feelings. He knew he shouldn't have come, but he was glad to have played a part. Besides, the celebrations were fun and he was enjoying all the attention.

Merryn tightened her grip on Kester's hand. She wanted to lead a normal life with her parents and friends, but the thought of never returning to this beautiful land filled her with a huge empty ache. It was as if she belonged with wizards who were on the side of all that was good and true. As for Kester, how could she bear to leave him when they'd shared so much?

The journey back to The Portal passed in a daze. The Great Wizard took Jake in his arms. Tobias took Hamish and Kester lifted Merryn. As they rose into the air they looked down on clear skies and the most beautiful of lands. They swooped low over the city and the people cheered and waved until they were out of sight and out of hearing.

The rest of the journey passed all too quickly and almost before they knew it, they were standing on the hilltop on Kerrera—three wizards and three children with Rex asleep at their feet. Jake flung his arms round his dog's neck and Rex licked his face in greeting.

A stray tear ran down Merryn's cheek.

'Do not be sad,' said Kester.

'I can't help it,' she said. 'I'm glad we put an end to The Grand High Witch and The Snake Wand. I'm glad The Stone Spell is broken. I'm glad The Malevolent Witches are dead, but... I don't think I'll ever see you again.'

Kester cupped her chin in his hands and tilted her face. 'What will be will be. We must accept it, but wherever we are and whatever we do, we will be linked in the fight against evil. That will never stop. For my people it will go on for ever and ever.'

'I know,' said Merryn, 'and I'll try to do the same. The witches may have gone but there are other things wrong in the world. Perhaps I can use The Gift to make Earth into a better place.'

'I fear that your task is greater than mine,' he said. 'Your world is changing fast and neither of us can see the future. No one can, not even wizards.'

Merryn gave a wry smile. 'It still makes me sad though, thinking that our adventures together are over.'

'I feel it too,' he said, 'but we must be happy with what we have shared. It has been a wonderful experience, a journey filled with fear and unimaginable horrors. But we have come through unharmed and there has been the joy of knowing one another.'

Merryn dashed another tear away. 'And now you have to go home. I'm glad I've been to your land, glad to know how beautiful it is, and glad to have known so many of your people. I'll be able to close my eyes and remember every little detail.'

'As I will close mine and remember you,' said Kester.

The Great Wizard smiled. 'Such encounters come but once in a lifetime or not at all. When they do occur they are too precious to forget.' He touched a strand of Merryn's hair. 'I will remember you as I remember your great-great-great-great grandmother, the first Merryn MacQueen of long ago.'

He shook hands with each of them in turn. 'Farewells between good friends are hard to bear, but this one cannot be avoided. Your journey and the reason for it has been the most important event in the history of my people. It will be written down in The Annals of Benevolent Wizardry. Our poets will write of it, our minstrels will sing of it and our people will tell of the three children who travelled from the planet Earth to save our land and our people. From now until the end of time, you will be remembered.'

AFTERWORD

Merryn glanced at her watch. The numbers were changing. Time had already moved on.

'All that in no time at all,' she said with a sigh.

She looked up at the sky. There was nothing to break the blue, no clouds, no sign of wizards wending their way back to The Land of Benevolent Wizardry.

'Not even a second lost,' said Hamish, 'and I don't care what time it is. I'm starving. I feel as if I haven't eaten for a week.'

'You haven't,' said Jake.

All three of them laughed as they remembered the days that had passed without feelings of hunger or thirst, long days that were outside the time that governed life on Earth.

They sat on the hilltop, took out their packed lunches and gazed over the island of Kerrera to the sea.

'So what do we do now?' asked Jake.

'Forget about magic,' said Hamish. 'No more looking for witches.'

'But we've got to do something,' said Merryn. 'There are still seven of us. We can be like the wizards. We can try to do things that make a difference.'

'Like what?' Jake asked.

'Stopping litter louts for a start,' she said as she grabbed a crisp packet that was in danger of blowing away. 'There are lots of things that need to change. I'll make a list and then we can decide where to start. We must meet the others too. They'll want to know everything that happened. Besides,' she gave an

245

impish grin, 'if the Travel Magic still works, there's no end to the places we can visit.'

'Or what we can do when we get to them,' said Hamish. 'It sounds brilliant, but I'm going to enjoy Kerrera first.' He stuffed his empty lunch box into his rucksack and leapt to his feet. 'Come on, I'll race you to Gylen Castle. This time I'm going to invent a game that doesn't have witches in it.'

He set off with Jake and Rex, careering down the hill, whooping delightedly. Merryn watched them go. She was in no hurry. She would finish her lunch in peace and then she'd follow at her own pace. Besides, she wanted to hang on to the memory of her last few hours with Kester. She wanted to ponder on all that had happened in The Land of Benevolent Wizardry. She didn't think she'd forget a moment of it, but just in case, she'd write it all down.

'That's what I'll do,' she said aloud. 'I'll write about our adventures. I'll start at the very beginning when I first heard the cry at midnight and I'll tell everything that happened, right up to this very minute.'

As she wandered down the slope of Carn Breugach she smiled to herself. It would be the most magical adventure story, and no one would guess that every single word was true.

THE HAGSTONE CHRONICLES
BOOK ONE—*CRY AT MIDNIGHT* by Mavis Gulliver
Published by Cinnamon Press, July 2014

On their first night in Aunt Aggie's cottage on the Hebridean Isle of Tiree, Merryn and Hamish MacQueen begin an exciting but terrifying adventure.

Inside a carved box Merryn finds a necklace of sea-beans and hag-stones. This allows her to see magical creatures and encloses her in a bubble that cannot be penetrated by witches. She also discovers that she has inherited The Gift from her great-great-great-great grandmother, another Merryn MacQueen of long ago. The Gift allows her to connect with magical beings, but it also means that she is honour-bound to join the fight against evil.

With her brother's help she embarks on a mission to save a horse called Kester. Trapped in a fencepost by a witch, Kester can be released by Merryn between midnight and sunrise. Riding through successive nights, she and Hamish are hindered by Aunt Maggie's strict rules and the witch's powerful spells.

Selkies and Fairy Folk pledge their help, but not until seemingly impossible challenges have been met. The adventure takes the children to the Ringing Stone and the beach of Traigh nan Gilean, but will Kester finally be freed and what is his true identity?

THE HAGSTONE CHRONICLES
BOOK TWO—*CLICKFINGER* by Mavis Gulliver
Published by Cinnamon Press, May 2015

Merryn and Hamish MacQueen think that a cottage on the tiny island of Kerrera will be the perfect place to spend their summer. There are wild goats and otters, beaches, cliffs, caves and the ruins of a castle.

To Hamish, their adventure on Tiree is as vague as a dream. To Merryn it is as clear as if it happened yesterday. She could never forget the horse that called at midnight or the challenges she had to face. Most of all she remembers Kester. Her dearest wish is to see him again, but the chances of that are very remote.

She treasures the crystal that he gave her. The necklace of sea-beans and hag-stones still hangs round her neck, but since the death of the Tiree witch it has been silent. On their very first day on Kerrera everything changes. The necklace begins to throb...

Malevolent Witchery is growing. Tobias and Kester Witchbane have returned to The Land of Benevolent Wizardry, but Merryn is expected to contact them if another witch appears.

Led by The Grand High Witch and The Snake Wand, huge numbers of witches are trying to destroy everything that is good and true. Disguised as ordinary women with ordinary jobs they turn up in the most unexpected places. Where and in what form will they appear next?

So begins an adventure that is even more perilous than the last. There are many children involved. All of them are in danger and only Merryn has the power to save them.